# THE BAKER STREET MYSTERIES

## The
## Rose of Africa

D0493807

TIM PIGOTT-SMITH

Illustrated by Chris Mould

Hodder
Children's
Books

A division of Hachette Children's Books

Typeset in Garamond by Avon DataSet Ltd,
Bidford on Avon, Warwickshire

Printed in the UK by CPI Bookmarque, Croydon, CR0 4TD

The paper and board used in this paperback by Hodder Children's Books
are natural recyclable products made from wood grown in
sustainable forests. The manufacturing processes conform to the
environmental regulations of the country of origin.

Hodder Children's Books
a division of Hachette Children's Books
338 Euston Road, London NW1 3BH
An Hachette UK company
www.hachette.co.uk

*To Pam and Tom*

*My thanks to Jeremy Pragnell, Peter Richardson,*
*John Lloyd and Peter Rook for help on jewellery,*
*medical publications, Victorian detail and legal help,*
*in that order!*

# PROLOGUE

'Titch! Jump!'

Clinging to the back of a hansom-cab, Sam Wiggins and Titch Simpson were bumming a free ride to Baker Street. The driver spotted them as they were passing through Marylebone. He was furious and turned on them. They leaped off and scooted down the road, followed by the driver who was so incensed that he deserted his cab and gave chase, cursing and cracking his whip.

Sam and Titch got well ahead of him and reached a big house at the centre of a crescent. Bounding over the railings, they nipped down the front steps and took cover in the basement. They had noticed before that this grand house, unlike all the others in the crescent, had no gate, and they had earmarked it as a possible hiding-place. While they were waiting for the cab-driver to give up his pursuit, they discovered something extraordinary.

The whole thing was a sham. The basement windows they were looking at were not real windows, and the door in front of which they were hiding was not a proper door. It did not open. It was not supposed to.

This door was not hinged, but nailed in place. Sam and Titch eventually managed to prise it open, and behind it they discovered a passageway. It was dark, but not in the least musty or airless. They followed it cautiously, and came upon huge air vents which connected to the underground railway below – they could hear the trains, rumbling by beneath their feet. Sam and Titch had stumbled on the secret of the house in the centre of the crescent – it was no more than a facade to conceal an ugly but essential service building.

They were looking for a new home. Limehouse, with its slimy alleyways and dark mouldy corners, was a loathsome place, and after the narrow escape of their friend Ann-li and their fear of revenge from the Dragon Clan of Shanghai, the Isle of Dogs held too many dangers for them. They had tried out different parts of London – Borough, Spitalfields – without settling anywhere. Then, by chance, they came across the phony door. Off the passage it concealed, they found a forgotten room with some rusty tools in one corner. This room became their new hideaway, and they guarded its secret with their lives.

In their haven – which had perhaps been a workman's store – their furnishings were sparse, but they smuggled some scraps of carpet down there, and Mrs Hudson contributed a couple of old army blankets that Dr Watson no longer used. Sam made a shelf – a bit of wood and two bricks – where he kept his growing library of medical books, and found a safe place to hide his sock of slowly growing savings. Titch still kept her few possessions – photographs and letters from her uncle in Calcutta – in her old shoulder bag – the one she had brought with her when she'd run away from home.

There was one object of which Sam took special care: a horseshoe, wrapped in red cloth. Edie had presented it to him, explaining that it was a well-known London charm to ward off nightmares. Sam was touched by her thoughtful gift, and sometimes when he was disturbed by a bad dream, he just lay there clutching it; it comforted him.

One night, Sam woke, screaming. Titch shuffled across and spoke gently to him. 'Ssssh! Sam! It's just a dream. It's not real. Sssssssh.' Sam was sweating and panicky, and it took Titch some time to quieten him. 'Shall I light the candle, Sam?'

'Yeah. Thanks.'

Titch had picked up Sam's anxiety and fumbled with the matches. 'Have you got the horseshoe, Sam?'

'Yeah.'

'What was the dream?'

'The usual.'

'The chase?'

'I don't think I'll ever get over it, Titch.'

'It was years ago, though, Sam. You haven't had to steal for ages.'

'I know. But it was terrifying. I thought I'd never get away.'

'You did, though. Think of that.'

For a moment, Sam was relieved. He almost smiled. 'That was the night I bumped into Mr Holmes and Dr Watson.'

'Funny that, ain't it?'

'Funny to think we know them now.'

'Ay. Nice bloke, the doctor.'

'You gotta look out for a little boat, you know, Titch. He'll buy it for you. I know he will.'

'I think I might have found something.'

'Good. He hasn't got a clue you're a girl, you know. No one has.' They chuckled.

'I'm not so sure,' Titch admitted. 'But it don't matter now.'

'No. And I like the doc,' said Sam. 'You know where you are with him.'

'Not like Mr Holmes.'

'No. Nor my blasted nightmares.'

'Eh?'

'You know how they usually follow the same pattern? I think I've got away and then there he is – the pursuer – smack in front of me. He nearly gets me when I have to climb over the wall, then I can't move because the ground's all sticky like? You know?' Titch nodded. 'Well sometimes, now, it's different.'

'Like what?'

'Like I'll find myself not just running away, but drowning or suffocating. And then it gets dead scary again.'

'You were screaming tonight, Sam. You woke me up.'

'It was the worst I've ever known it.' Sam was cold now, but still drenched with sweat. Titch was frightened too, but she tried to make Sam feel better by telling him again that it was just a dream. Sam agreed

– a dream was only a dream. But whatever reassurances Titch gave him, Sam still felt afraid, and fear was fear – *that* was real. And it wouldn't go away.

'Titch.'

'Yeah?'

'Thanks.'

'What for? I ain't done nowt.'

'Just for being here. You all right?'

'Ay. You scared me.'

'Come here.' Sam pushed the horseshoe down underneath his blanket, and opened his arm. Titch put her head on his shoulder. Sometimes when they were afraid like this, they lay together, clinging to each other – like brother and sister – two waifs against the world.

'I don't know what I'd do without you, Titch.'

'Nor me,' said Titch. 'You're the best thing that ever happened to me.'

'Titch, you know how you're scared that your dad'll turn up one day, looking for you?'

'Ay.'

'Well, I don't think he ever will. It's all in the mind – like my dream.'

'I know.'

'So we're both scared of things that don't exist.'

'Ay. Daft really.'

'Tell you what though, Titch.'

'What?'

'We'll be all right if we stick together.'

'I know.'

'So . . . will you?'

'You know I will, Sam.'

'Promise?'

'Promise.'

'Me too.'

They lay, silent and close for some time. Then Titch whispered, 'Can you face the dark now, Sam?'

'Yeah. I reckon. Thanks.'

Titch leaned up on one elbow and blew the candle out.

# 1

# UNCLE HECTOR

Billy Chizzell, the page-boy at 221b Baker Street, stood in the hall, waiting for the storm to break. His friend, Sam Wiggins, who had dropped in to see him, watched with him.

'What's going on, Billy?'

'Some nob's been to see Mr Holmes. Real posh. Foreign accent.'

'Oh, him. I saw him leaving just now in a fancy carriage.'

'Looks like European royalty to me,' said Billy. 'I fancy the guv'nor will be leaving shortly too, so I've taken the precaution of having a hansom-cab stand by. Where's Titch?'

'In the kitchen with Mrs Hudson.'

'Leftovers of a nice cinnamon tart today!'

The two lads were looking up the stairs to Sherlock Holmes's study when suddenly the door burst open.

'Billy!' came Holmes's cry. 'Order me a cab!'

Billy turned to Sam. 'What did I tell you?'

Sam grinned. 'Clever old you.'

Holmes was shouting. 'Goodbye, Watson! I must away. This mission is top secret. My presence is urgently required!' When he had something on his mind, Holmes was like a man possessed. He swept out of his study, almost knocking Dr Watson over. He continued his frantic descent of the staircase, donning his Aberdeen cape and deerstalker hat as he went.

'Get my luggage!' he roared at Billy, who dodged him, running *up* the stairs to collect Holmes's portmanteau. 'Out of my way, Wiggins! There will be no need for you and the team on this assignment!' cried Holmes as he ran to the door and flung it open. He would have charged straight out, but his path was barred by a scruffy young lad wearing a battered bowler. It was the wiry figure of Potts, who was usually game for a laugh, but on this occasion was out of breath, and looking decidedly green.

'Potts!' cried Holmes with surprise. 'What are you doing here? I have already told Wiggins the Irregulars are surplus to requirements on this case. Out of my way!'

'I need your 'elp, Mr 'Olmes,' panted Potts. 'I 'ate to ask, but you gotta 'elp me!'

'I beg your pardon, Potts. I have not a moment to spare.'

'But Mr 'Olmes, it's dead serious. Please. You gotta just 'ear me out.'

Holmes pushed past Potts, making straight for the hansom that Billy had ordered. The cab horse stamped as if to warm himself against the cold mist of a winter afternoon.

'Waterloo Station!' Holmes bellowed at the driver. 'With all haste!'

As Holmes was mounting the cab steps, Billy arrived, breathless, with his portmanteau.

Without a word of thanks, Holmes grabbed it from him and called again to the driver. 'Waterloo, my man. I *must* catch the boat-train!' The driver raised his whip, and the horse began to pull away.

Potts was jumping up and down, shouting, trying to get Holmes's attention. From the doorway, Sam, who had been joined by Billy and Dr Watson, watched in astonishment as Potts leaped on to the step of the moving hansom, preventing Holmes from closing the cab door. They could hear Potts pleading and see Holmes gesticulating.

Billy turned to Sam. 'What's going on?'

'I dunno,' replied Sam.

They all watched as the hansom-cab sped down Baker Street.

'What the heck happened while I was getting the bag, Sam?' asked Billy.

'Potts turned up. He was in a real state. Said he wanted Mr Holmes's help.'

'He'll be lucky!' Billy remarked.

The hansom was moving fast now. As it swung round the corner into the Marylebone Road, it looked as though Potts would be flung to the ground. However, as the cab disappeared into the thickening fog, they saw Holmes reach out, draw Potts inside and slam the door.

'He *was* lucky,' said Sam dryly. 'Not like Potts to be in such a stew.'

'I wonder what he wanted!' puffed Watson.

The three of them looked at each other.

'Yes,' said Billy. 'I wonder.'

Although he was angry with Potts, Holmes was equally curious. 'Damn you, Potts. What is it you want?' Potts was unable to speak. 'Get your breath back and tell me. We do not have long. Faster, driver, faster!' yelled

Holmes, thumping the roof of the cab to get the driver's attention. Potts felt he had been sucked into a whirlpool, but launched into his tale.

'Well, Mr H, it's like this. 'Ave you 'eard of the Rose of Africa?'

'Indeed I have, Potts. It is one of the largest pink diamonds in the world – the most valuable stone ever to come out of the Kimberley mines of South Africa. It is pear-shaped, weighs 125.02 carats – enormous – and is fabled to emit a pink glow.'

'Cor blimey, you know everyfing! Well, sir, it's been nicked.'

'That is hardly a surprise, Potts. It is of great beauty and inestimable value. What is harder to comprehend is why *you* should be telling me, and why its loss should so upset you. At least it might explain why you have been to Pentonville Prison.'

Potts was stunned. ''Ow do you know I've been to Pentonville?'

'The mud on the instep of your left boot is peculiar to that part of London. Tell me quickly why you are so distraught.'

The hansom-cab rattled round the corner into Gower Street, swaying violently. Clinging on for dear life, Potts continued with his tale.

'Well, sir, it's like this. The Rose was placed in one of the safety deposit boxes at the African Diamond Company in Mayfair. It's vanished. Gone. I know cos my Uncle 'Ector works there. Leastways 'e *did*. But they've been and gone and arrested '*im* for nickin' it. Well anyone 'oo knows my Uncle 'Ector knows that 'e couldn't 'ave done it. 'E's not the type. Steady as you like, my uncle – this was 'is bowler by the way, wot 'e give me.' Potts was very fond of his Uncle Hector's old bowler hat, and as he spoke of it, he took it off and stroked it lovingly.

'Get on with it, Potts.'

'Sorry. Well, 'Ector don't drink. 'E practically lives down Temperance Hall – always singing hymns and bashin' away at 'is bloomin' tambourine, 'e is. Drives us nuts. 'E simply would not do a fing like this.'

'I believe you, Potts, but this constitutes no defence at all. You need evidence.'

'It gets worse, tho', Mr H.'

'Do tell me – and quickly – we are approaching Covent Garden.' Holmes was leaning forward with his chin on his hands. His eyes were intent on Potts, and his mind concentrated on the young boy's story.

'It's like this, sir. The Shift Manager – 'oo was a friend of 'Ector's – is found dead in the vaults.'

'Of the African Diamond Company?'

'Of the African Diamond Company. Exactly. And – 'ere comes the dodgy bit – they find 'Ector standin' over the body.'

'Oh dear, Potts.'

'It gets worse. In 'is pocket they find a ticket. It's for a one-way steamboat trip to South Africa. Don't look good, do it?'

'It looks very bleak indeed, Potts.'

'It gets worse. On the dead body was the very gun wot the Shift Manager 'ad been shot wiv. When Inspector Lestrade arrives at the murder scene, 'e asks 'Ector 'oo done it. And 'Ector says, "Me!" It's dopey. No one believes 'im.'

'Where was the the Rose?'

'Gone. Not there.'

Holmes drew breath. Then he asked Potts, 'Can you by any chance describe the murder weapon to me?'

'I can actually, sir. When we were up at Pentonville to see 'Ector, Inspector Lestrade told us it was quite small. More of a pistol, like. Wiv a pearl 'andle.'

'A pistol with a pearl handle?' Holmes sat back pensively in his seat. 'Potts, your uncle is quite clearly innocent.'

'Wot about the steamer ticket?'

'Irrelevant.'

'Wot about the pearl- 'andled pistol?'

'Circumstantial piffle.'

'Wot about 'im admitting it, Mr H?'

'A cover. I am confident, Potts, that your uncle will be cleared of all charges. Unless, of course, that fool Lestrade believes him.'

'I can't let 'Ector go to the gallows for sumfing 'e never done. 'E's a lovely man.'

'Waterloo Bridge. We shall soon be there,' remarked Holmes peering through the cab window.

'Wot can I do to 'elp 'im, Mr H?'

'You must find out *why* your uncle is lying, Potts. Fear of the gallows may well loosen his tongue.'

'You don't know 'Ector. When 'e's set on sumfing a team of 'orses can't shift 'im. And 'e's loyal to a fault.'

'My dear Potts, you will find that nothing focuses the mind quite like death. Here we are. Waterloo Station. Forgive me, I must leave you.' So saying, Holmes took up his portmanteau. Without another word to Potts, he opened the cab door and leaped out, throwing the cab-driver a handful of coins as he did so. Potts watched him bound across the pavement and up the steps. As Holmes disappeared among the press of people, Potts was obliged to get out of the cab. The tired horse was steaming in the biting cold. Walking home to Soho, Potts contemplated Holmes's advice.

'Circumstantial piffle?' he said to himself. 'Fanks for nuffing, Mr 'Olmes!'

Back at Baker Street, the atmosphere was muted – it nearly always was when Sherlock Holmes was away on business. When Edie had sold all her herbs, she joined Billy, Sam and Titch, and the four of them sat listlessly in the kitchen, getting under Mrs Hudson's feet, debating where Holmes might have gone. Edie was noticeably quiet – she was worried about Potts.

Billy had seen a royal crest on an envelope, and he was convinced that his master was helping a royal family in Europe: whenever there was a dynastic problem anywhere on the continent, Holmes was summoned.

'You're right, Billy,' added Sam. 'He was aiming to get the boat-train from Waterloo.'

They talked this over, and cleaned up what little Titch had left of Mrs Hudson's cinnamon tart. When Dr Watson returned from his evening surgery, the Irregulars tried to persuade him to tell them where Holmes had gone, but Watson had been sworn to secrecy. It was while they were trying to prise this news out of Watson that Potts returned, looking paler than ever, accompanied by his father, who was still wearing his police uniform.

'I think we had better get out of Mrs Hudson's way, and go upstairs, don't you?' said Watson.

'If I'm ever to get this kitchen tidy, I think you had,' said Mrs Hudson sharply. 'Go on. Off you go.'

In the study there was plenty of room, and they soon forgot about Holmes as they listened to Potts and his dad recounting their visit to Uncle Hector at Pentonville that morning.

'Pentonville Prison,' said Potts, 'is the vilest place I've ever been.'

'That's cos you ain't been inside Newgate, son,' said Mr Potts gloomily.

'It still gives yer the creeps, Dad. And seeing Uncle H in that bloomin' uniform – it's like sumfing out the Penny Dreadfuls.'

'How *is* Uncle Hector?' enquired Edie.

'They've got him pickin' oakum or something half the day,' said Potts glumly. 'It's 'orrible. You tell 'em, Dad.'

'Well the real problem is my bloomin' brother. We know he's not guilty but he insists he is. Potts offered to get Mr Holmes to help out, but Hector don't want to know. *"I don't need Sherlock Holmes,"* he says. *"I'm guilty!"* Stupid duffer's made up his mind to go through with it for some reason.'

'For some reason,' said Sam under his breath.

'Sure, if he says he's guilty, they'll hang him, won't they, Potts?' asked Edie.

Potts nodded. 'They've got this gallows up there in a shed. There's a pit underneath it. It's 'orrible, Edie. The thought of dear old Uncle 'Ector in there . . . wiv a rope round 'is neck and an 'ood over 'is 'ead . . .' Potts could not continue. None of them spoke, as they contemplated Uncle Hector going to the gallows.

Eventually, Billy asked what Inspector Lestrade's attitude was. Mr Potts pointed out that although Lestrade had a body on his hands, which was a concern, he also had someone admitting to the murder. They were all agreed that Lestrade wouldn't lift a finger to help Hector unless he was forced to.

'What about the diamond?' asked Titch.

'Good point, Titch,' said Sam. 'What about the Rose, Mr Potts?'

'It's gone. Vanished.'

'But if Hector took it,' Sam persisted, 'why didn't he have it *on* him when they found him with the body?'

'That's the mystery,' said Mr Potts.

''E won't talk about it,' said Potts. ''E's lying, though. You can tell.'

'Did he give it to someone?' asked Billy.

'That's wot we reckon, but 'e won't say,' said Potts with frustration. 'If there's anyfing 'e don't like the sound of, 'e just clams up. You can't shift 'im.'

Mr Potts shrugged. 'Lestrade *says* he's got a couple of bobbies out there looking for the Rose, but they don't stand a chance. It's probably out the country already. Nobody's gonna try and sell it, not in London – it's too well known.'

'Was Mr Holmes any help, Potts?' Edie enquired.

'Not really, Edie. That's why we come 'ere – in the 'ope that *we* might do sumfin' – the Irregulars. All Mr H said was to find out *why* 'Ector is lying. And that the whole fing was based on "circumstantial piffle" and 'Ector'd be found innocent in the end.'

'It's all right for him in flipping Ruritania,' said Billy. 'It's not the guv'nor who's going to swing, is it?'

''E said the fear of death would probably loosen 'Ector's tongue,' said Potts.

'He don't know my brother, does he, son?'

'No, Dad. 'E don't.'

They all fell quiet again. Watson had been observing

the Irregulars. He was impressed by their closeness, and liked the intelligent way they sifted through the problem. The five of them formed a remarkable team. Watson particularly admired Sam – the thoughtful one. Sam had been withdrawn for some time, but at this moment, he leaned forward and placed his chin on his hands, reminding Watson of Holmes. With huge concentration, Sam asked, 'What exactly did Mr Holmes dismiss as "circumstantial piffle", Potts?'

'The pistol wot they found on the body.'

Sam thought for a moment. Dr Watson pointed out that according to the evening papers – which were full of the story – it was a *pearl-handled* pistol.

'That's right, Dr W,' said Potts.

'Yes, it's interesting,' observed Sam. 'But what really intrigues me is the other question.'

'Why Hector's lying, you mean?'

'Exactly, Titch. "For *some* reason," you said, Mr Potts. Well . . . for *what* reason?'

'We don't know. That's what he won't say.'

'Then that's what we have to find out. Do you mind if I ask you what kind of a person Hector is, Mr Potts?'

'Too bloomin' good to be true,' replied Mr Potts. 'Always was. Never drank. Never smoked. Never swore. Drove me barmy – I was always in trouble.' He filled

22

them in on Hector's religious convictions, and his work at Temperance Hall, campaigning to stop people drinking alcohol. He had held the job at the African Diamond Company ever since its foundation nearly ten years ago, hardly missing a day's work in all that time. He had never been in trouble with his employers. He had never been in debt. He had never got on the wrong side of the law. It seemed more and more extraordinary that such a model brother should find himself in his present mess.

'What does his wife say about all this?' asked Sam.

'He don't have one,' replied Mr Potts. 'He's never had one.'

'Oh, sorry,' said Sam, feeling a bit embarrassed.

'In fact, now you mention it, Sam, it's the only area where he's gone off the tracks at all, and even then it's not his fault, like.'

'What do you mean, Mr Potts?'

Potts's dad explained that Hector was a complete romantic when it came to women. He had been involved with two women in his time, both wildly unsuitable. Hector had loved them to distraction, and both had taken advantage of the poor man – one had disappeared with most of his money.

'Ah. I see,' said Sam. 'Now I get it.'

'What?' said Titch.

'Yeah, what?' cried Billy.

'I see why Mr Holmes dismissed the evidence as circumstantial piffle.'

'How come?' asked Mr Potts.

'Well,' said Sam, 'Hector's lying, isn't he?' There was general agreement. 'I think he's lying because of a woman.'

'What makes you think there was a woman involved?' asked Mr Potts.

'There's no evidence of a woman at all, Sam!' cried the others.

'But I think there is,' Sam insisted.

'Wot?' asked Potts.

'Show us the evidence!' cried Billy.

'The murder weapon,' said Sam.

'What about it?' asked Billy.

Sam was calm and deliberate. 'The gun has a pearl handle, doesn't it, Potts?'

'Yeah.'

'"Small pistol" it says in the paper –' said Titch, '– just the right size for a woman to slip into her handbag sort of thing.'

'Exactly, Titch. Wouldn't a woman be more likely to own a small pistol with a pearl handle than a man?'

They all thought about this for a moment.

'You're right, Sam,' they agreed.

'The point is,' Sam continued, 'Uncle Hector is lying for a reason. Right? If the reason is *to protect a woman*, it would all make sense, wouldn't it?'

'It would, Sam,' said Potts. 'You're dead bloomin' right! So . . . it's shershay la fam, innit?'

'What does that mean?' asked Edie.

'Shershay la fam is a French expression, Edie,' said Potts with a smirk.

'I know that, Potts. I just don't know what it means.'

'It means find the bird, don' it, Dr W?'

'Or to be strictly accurate, Edie,' said Watson with a smile, '*cherchez la femme* means *find the woman*.'

'Find the bird! Like I said!' beamed Potts, pleased as punch. 'There's one behind every crime, Edie. Specially in France. That's all we have to do now, my friends, to get 'Ector off the 'ook! Find the flippin' bird!'

# 2
# FIND THE BIRD!

That very evening the Irregulars got to work. They needed to know more about Uncle Hector and his recent past. According to Mr Potts, the man to see was Alf Jenx, Hector's closest friend and fellow stalwart at Temperance Hall in Southwark. Edie and Potts set out to find him.

Sam felt that if they stood any chance at all of tracing the Rose of Africa, they should also know something about the world of precious gems. At his urgent request, Dr Watson went straight to his club to contact an old army chum who had stayed on in India to work in diamond mining – then a developing industry. Watson often told the story of how his friend had once been given a huge diamond and put it in his waistcoat pocket. 'He forgot clean about it! Sent the waistcoat to the laundry six weeks later, and his dhobi found it!' Watson was sure that his old friend, who was so wealthy he had retired, and whom he saw regularly at the club, would provide Sam with the entrée he needed.

Sam and Titch stayed behind at Baker Street: Watson would not be back till late; Potts and Edie would report back from Temperance Hall at lunchtime the next day; Billy had gone home to his mum. They pored over the newspaper reports of the robbery and murder, and when they had read everything they could find, they slipped off to their hideaway and talked till late about Hector and diamonds.

At his club, Watson met up with his friend, who wrote a name and address on the back of his visiting-card and assured Watson that all he had to do was present the card, for Sam to learn everything he needed to know about jewellery. So, next morning, Watson took Sam to London's diamond district. Sam's eyes were on stalks as they walked down Hatton Garden. He didn't notice the cold as they passed heavily protected shop windows glistening with necklaces, bracelets, rings and chokers. Sam could see silver, gold and gems of all sorts – rubies, emeralds, amethysts and, of course, diamonds.

'It's another world, isn't it, Dr Watson?' said Sam, in wonder.

'It is, Sam. Another world.'

Towards the end of Hatton Garden, they took a narrow passageway into Ely Place – home of the recently formed London Diamond Syndicate, an imposing building behind locked carriage gates, attended by liveried guards.

'What's that, Dr Watson?' Sam enquired.

'The syndicate represents all the diamond merchants of London, Sam. A very important place. They control prices.'

Just past the gates was an inconspicuous shop set back in a corner. It looked so dowdy and neglected that they almost missed it. There was condensation on the small panes of glass in the door, and the bow window needed a good clean. This unlikely venue was the address to which the visiting card directed them. After the extravagance of the more opulent shops he had been gawping at, Sam's spirits fell. Watson didn't say anything, but he was also somewhat taken aback as he mounted the two worn steps to ring the bell. After a moment the door was unbolted, unlocked and nudged open by a wizened old man. The skin around his eyes was deeply lined, but Sam couldn't see much of his face because thick grey hair fell forward on to his forehead. A large, unkempt grey beard covered his cheeks and chin. His spectacles had thick round lenses. Through the narrow gap in the door, he looked down suspiciously at Watson.

'Yes? Vot you vant?'

'Mr Curtis?' Watson asked doubtfully. Sam didn't think he looked like a Mr Curtis at all.

'Ruben Curtis, yes.' His accent was strong – when he said Ruben, the 'r' was thick and guttural.

'My name is Watson. A friend of mine – ex-Major Grantham – said I should give you this.' Watson handed him the visiting-card. The old man peered at it closely, and his hostile manner changed instantly.

'You are *Doctor* Vatson?' he asked, offering Watson his hand. 'Often the Major speaks of you. A friend of his is also a friend of mine. Come in. Please. Vot is your name, boy?'

'Sam, sir.'

'Ah. Samuel. A good Jewish name,' he said chuckling. 'Come in, come in.' As he ushered them inside, Sam noticed that he was wearing a small Jewish skullcap. His tired trousers and waistcoat were black and he had on a pair of soft knitted slippers. He was in shirt-sleeves, and wore a work apron. 'Close the door, Samuel. That's my boy.'

Sam and Watson found themselves in a cluttered shop, with a stove burning away merrily, making it as warm as toast. There was a counter and a display case, but Sam could barely make out what was in it, because the only light, apart from that which filtered thinly through the grimy windows, came from above the workbench in the corner by the stairs. Here Sam could see a piece of black velvet, on which were clustered three or four small mounds of gleaming gems. Ruben pushed his stool close to the workbench, sat down and asked, 'Vot can I do for you?'

Sam explained that he wanted a crash course in diamonds. The old man grinned at Watson, and asked if it was a good time for Sam to stay right now.

'Yes, please, Mr Curtis, sir!' cried Sam. 'Perfect!'

Watson smiled, made his goodbyes and set off for his surgery. Sam found himself alone with Ruben Curtis, jeweller. Ruben pushed his glasses on to his forehead and picked up an eye-piece. 'This is called a loupe,' he said, bending over the piles of gems. 'It magnifies ten times.' He indicated to Sam to watch as he sorted the stones, picking each one up with a large pair of tweezers and turning it carefully. Sam was intrigued.

'What are you looking for, sir?'

'I look to see if there are any inclusions in them, Samuel.'

'What's an inclusion?'

'Imperfections. Shall ve start at the beginning?'

'Yes, please, sir.'

As Ruben worked, he talked. 'Vell, the vord diamond is from the Greek "adamas" which means invincible – the diamond *is* invincible – it's the hardest known mineral there is. It's vot ve call an allotrope of carbon, but let's not get too technical. It's tough, Samuel – that's vot matters. It can cut glass, it's so tough.'

Sam listened as Ruben explained how diamonds were created, and how they are grouped into 'cleavages' – 'that's the splittability, Samuel,' – 'macles' and 'flats', in order to help price them. He continued to pick up the stones, one at a time, examining them intensely under the light, exploring each one from every angle possible. 'The thing about diamonds, Samuel, is that you never know vot you may find. Vot ve got here is a bag of rough – uncut stones. They may be nuthink – they *look* very ordinary – but you never know. You have to search the heart of each vun, and there you may find . . .'

'What, sir?'

'That's just it – you don't know till you see it. Beauty. Vealth.' He smiled. 'Beauty, that's the drug. You *have* to look, because maybe, just maybe . . . in this little gem that has come to me all the way from the diamond mines of Asia vere it took millions of years to form in the bowels of the earth – in here, you might just find the answer to all your dreams.'

Listening to Ruben, Sam quite lost track of the time. It was lunch-time when the old man locked the shop and set him on the route home. They went up Hatton Garden, passing again the sparkling shops that had entranced Sam earlier.

'My lunch-time constitutional, Samuel. I hope our little talk vos useful.'

'Oh, yes. Thank you, sir.'

'Don't forget it, vill you?'

'Not likely!' Sam exclaimed.

They went up a slight incline and round the corner into Leather Lane. Here, the whole feel of the area changed immediately. The wealth and glamour of the jewellery shops were replaced by dilapidated red-brick tenements – one push, it seemed, would knock them down. Gone were the smart, suited shoppers of Hatton Garden, their places taken by grubby, ill-dressed, ill-mannered loutish people. As Ruben and

Sam passed The Shamrock – a down-at-heel pub – Ruben remarked, 'Filthy dump. I vould like to burn that place down.'

'Why?'

'You could learn how to do things the wrong vay in there. It's home to every fence, every flimp and schneider in London.'

'I don't know what schneider means, sir.'

'So you know vot a flimp is already?' said Ruben with mock horror.

Sam grinned. 'Everyone knows that – flimping is snatching something – stealing – but *schneider* . . . no, sir, I don't know that one.'

'Am I glad to hear that, my dear Samuel? Schneid means a counterfeit – you know, a copy, a fake. A schneider is the man who makes them – in other words – a villain! That pub is full of them. You'll be all right from here, Samuel. Please – come and see me any time.'

'Thank you, sir. Goodbye.'

Sam hurried back to Baker Street, his mind bursting with everything Ruben had told him. Titch and Billy were already there, with Potts and Edie, whose mission to Southwark had been successful – they had traced Hector's friend, Alf Jenx.

'Tell us what you found out,' said Billy.

'You done most o' the chat, Edie,' said Potts. 'You tell.'

Edie launched into an account of their talk. Alf confirmed everything they had learned about Hector from Potts's dad. Moreover, he was certain that Hector, who he said was completely reliable in all other respects, had got into his present difficulties because he had once again chosen the wrong woman.

'Did he give any details?' asked Billy, craning forward eagerly.

'One night, on the steps of Temperance Hall,' Edie continued, 'Hector encountered this woman. She was crying like a water cart, and Hector . . .'

''Oo's always been a sucker for a damsel in distress,' smirked Potts.

'. . . took care of her. Hector tells Alf everything, to be sure,' Edie went on, 'and this mysterious woman wove him a story of diamonds swindled from friends back in South Africa and how she was desperate to help them recover their stolen jewels.'

'Wow!' said Billy.

'Sure,' said Edie, 'Alf *never* trusted her.'

'Well, it's a fair old coincidence, innit?' added Potts. ''Er bumpin' into 'Ector, who just 'appens to work at the African Diamond Company! She must 'ave planned the whole fing.'

'Alf warned Hector,' Edie continued, 'but he wouldn't hear a word against her. He was besotted. He was dreaming of marriage, of emigrating to South Africa with her, of having his own farm. Like Alf said – "the works".'

'The question is,' said Sam, 'if this mystery woman is the woman that we think Hector is lying to protect, can we find her, and can we build a case around her that will get Hector off?'

The Irregulars depended on Sam to provide the answers, not the questions.

'You tell *us*, Sam,' Billy insisted.

'You're the gaffer!' said Potts.

'I'm thinking.'

'You always say that.'

'Well, Potts, I'm always thinking.'

'He is, too,' said Titch quietly. 'Give him a moment.'

'Sorry, Sam,' said Potts.

Sam collected himself. 'What's the *name* of Hector's mystery woman, Edie?'

'Adler. Irene Adler.'

'Spot on, Edie. Irene Adler.'

'So you see, Potts, it may not seem like it but

we're making progress.'

'Yeah I know. I'm just keen to get fings movin'.'

'Anyway,' said Titch, 'we don't know what *you* found out, Sam. You got any news?'

'I've got some stuff on the Rose. And I've learned quite a lot about diamonds, but I haven't got anything that will tell us where to start looking. That's why I'm thinking. But let me tell you about the jeweller.'

'Yeah. Tell us, tell us.'

'Wot's 'e like?'

'His name's Ruben Curtis – well, his real name is Kurtz, and he's from Russia. His family were persecuted because they were Jewish.' Potts was very quiet. His mum was Jewish but he preferred people not to know. 'They smuggled Ruben out when he was a boy – our age like,' Sam went on. 'The rest of his family were going to follow him but none of them made it. He's amazing. He knows everything about jewellery – silver, gold, diamonds, you name it. This is what he told me about the Rose.' Sam took a deep breath. 'You got to have this picture, see, of South Africa, and people making massive fortunes from diamond mining. Every now and then someone comes across a stone that's bigger and better and more valuable than anything that's ever come out the ground, and the Rose is one of them, yes?'

'I'd love to see it,' mused Edie.

'Me, too,' said Titch.

'Ruben showed me some things this morning that'd make your eyes water,' said Sam. 'So . . . The Rose belonged to this family who owned one of the mines – the Astons. They got into trouble somehow—'

'How?'

'They were bought out by a syndicate or something. It was a swindle. Anyway the thing is, the Astons lose everything. The only real wealth they have left is this one amazing stone – the Rose. Right?'

The Irregulars were now hanging on Sam's every word.

'What happened?'

'I bet it was nicked.'

'You're right, Potts. And the theft has this tragic effect on the Aston family. Mr Aston – who founded the diamond mine – he commits suicide.'

'Blimey.'

'Yeah. He shoots himself. And Mrs Aston can't cope – she dies not long after – a broken woman.' The Irregulars were somewhat subdued now, as Sam continued with his story of the Aston family. 'The two children end up with a small farmhouse and a bit of land – all that's left of the vast Aston estate – and a house here in London. The son survives by organising game-hunting safaris, but his younger sister is tipped over the edge by the whole thing, and she's now in a mental hospital.'

'They're horrible places,' said Titch. 'There's one down the Mile End Road. It's like a prison.'

''Oo nicked it, though? That's wot I wanna know,' asked Potts. ''Oo nicked the Rose?'

'A black houseboy of the Astons was convicted,' Sam answered, 'but the real suspect was some English lord. Sorry, Potts, this all takes time.'

'We ain't *got* time, tho' Sam. Poor old 'Ector goes up before the beak at the next session of the Bailey!'

'When's that?'

'Week tomorrow!'

'Wow!'

'If 'e tells 'em 'e's guilty, they'll take 'im straight back to Pentonville for the drop . . .' Potts made the sign of a noose snapping straight and jerked his head to one side. 'Goodbye, 'Ector. So can we please get shershaying la fam?'

'Listen. This time yesterday we didn't know anything at all, did we? And now at least we've got a fam to shershay, and I've got a theory.'

'Have you?' they all cried, relieved that their leader was not going to let them down.

'Yes, I have.'

'What? What is it?'

'Tell us, Sam.'

'I'm not sure it'll hold water,' said Sam cautiously, 'but this is what I'm thinking. When Hector met Miss Adler – his mystery woman – she spun him a yarn about diamonds stolen from her friends, the Astons – that's what Potts and Edie were told, right?' They nodded eagerly. 'Hector was so besotted, he couldn't see she was using him to get at the Rose . . .'

'That's 'Ector all right,' Potts chipped in miserably.

'. . . which was in the vaults of the African Diamond Company.'

The Irregulars were listening hard, following Sam's reasoning. Sam developed his theory that Hector – when he was on the night shift – agreed to let Miss Adler into the security room.

'He shouldn't have done it,' said Sam, 'but . . .'

'He wants to impress her,' commented Titch.

'Right. So . . . imagine he lets Miss Adler into the vaults – just to look at the Rose.'

'He's showing off,' added Edie.

'Or maybe he intends to steal it for her,' said Billy.

'Or for 'er friends,' added Potts.

'Maybe,' said Sam. 'So there they are in the vaults – Hector and Miss Adler. Picture it. It's late at night – they think they are alone. Maybe the deposit box is open. Maybe they're holding the Rose. Maybe *she* is holding the Rose. Yes?'

'Yes.'

'And they are surprised by the Shift Manager.'

'Who's on his rounds and just appears,' said Titch.

'The woman panics. She shoots him.'

'Why the woman?'

'Because, Titch, we suspect the pistol belongs to a woman, right?'

'Ay!'

'And she drops the pistol – in shock, like,' Sam continued.

'Yes?'

'Hector plays the big hero and persuades her to run for it . . .'

'*Wiv* the Rose,' cried Potts.

'That's how it vanished – *she* took it,' said Billy.

'. . . and Hector tells her he will cover for her.'

'Brilliant, Sam!' said Edie smiling.

'In the panic, her pistol is forgotten. It's on the body of the Shift Manager, who must have set the alarm off before entering the vaults,' Sam concluded, 'because the police arrive before Hector has a chance to invent a credible story, or dispose of the pistol. So he confesses. That's my theory,' said Sam. The Irregulars were excited now, and they all began talking at the same time.

'It's in character, Sam. 'Ector was always a soft touch.' – Potts.

'It explains why the pearl-handled pistol was on the body.' – Billy.

'Sure does.' – Edie.

'And how the Shift Manager was shot.' – Titch.

''Ow the Rose disappeared.' – Potts.

'Why Hector's got a steamer ticket to South Africa in his pocket.' – Billy.

'Because he's planning to emigrate and marry this Adler woman.' – Edie.

'Fantastic, Sam!' – Titch.

'Amazing!' – all of them.

'Don't get carried away, you lot,' said Sam, 'it's just a theory. We've still got to shershay Miss Adler.'

'I tell you sumfing,' said Potts. 'If you're right, Sam, and that's wot 'appened, and she done the murder and run off wiv the goods, I don't like the sound of 'er at all.'

They all agreed that if she was capable of shooting someone, and letting an innocent man go to the gallows for her, she was a pretty rum lot.

'She sounds calculating to me,' said Titch.

'Cruel.'

'Merciless.'

'*La Belle Dame Sans Merci*,' said Edie.

'You wot?'

'It's French, Potts.'

'I know that, Edie. I just don't know wot it means.'

'Sure, it means the Beautiful Lady with no Mercy.'

'Well, that's 'er, Edie. The lady wiv no mercy. When can we get shershay-ing then, Sam?'

'Just be patient, Potts.' Sam told them about a special library where they keep old newspapers. Dr Watson had promised to take Sam there so that he could read up on the theft of the Rose. 'I'm off there as soon as Dr Watson's free.'

'But you *know* about the theft, Sam.'

'Not the original theft from the Astons in South Africa, Potts.'

'You don't *need* to know, do you?'

'I just think the more information we have, the better off we'll be. Billy, you'd best hold the fort here. Right?'

'I should really.'

'Potts?'

'I'm runnin' for Mr Dyke – big undercover bare-knuckle fight on this afternoon – but I can 'elp out later.'

'Great. Titch, do you want to come with me?'

'I'm still working on that boat, Sam.'

'All right. Good luck. Edie, what about you?'

'Sure, I must go back to work, Sam – catch the afternoon rush hour.'

'Let's all be back here between six and seven, then, shall we?'

This met with general agreement.

'See you later, then,' said Sam.

'And let's 'ope we can make a bloomin' start on the old shershay, then! And find Miss Irene Adler!'

'Yes, Potts,' said Sam. 'Let's hope so.'

# 3

# THE LIE DETECTOR

D r Watson was mystified by Titch. Both he
and Holmes were convinced she was a girl,
and could not understand why the Irregulars
persisted with the myth of her being a boy. Perhaps
they didn't know! Watson well understood that when
Titch had run away from home it had been safer for
her to disguise herself but now it seemed unnecessary.
Watson wanted Titch to have a boat – he was familiar
with her background on the Manchester Ship Canal,
and she had handled the boat well during Ann-li's
rescue. The real point was that if Titch had her own
boat, she could earn an independent living, ferrying
passengers and parcels on the River Thames. While
Watson took Sam to the newspaper library, Titch
nipped over to Chelsea Wharf, where she had spotted

a tender for sale, moored to a houseboat. She tried to bargain, but the owner would not budge.

Titch was depressed. She wanted the boat, but thought it was overpriced. She walked back to 221b in low spirits. Sam opened the door.

'How d'you get on, Titch?'

'Too expensive.'

Sam did his best to cheer her up. 'Never mind. Keep trying. Something'll turn up.'

'I hope so. Are the others here?'

'Yeah. Billy's just popped out for the Doc's evening paper.'

As soon as Billy returned, the Irregulars gathered round the kitchen table, so that Sam could tell them what he had found out in the newspaper library.

'We have to go back to South Africa, where the Astons . . . Remember them?'

'Owners of the Rose.'

'That's them. Well, the Astons give this lavish party. The list of guests is incredible – a playboy prince from our royal family, a man known as the Great White Hunter, and an English lord name of Scarsbury. Lord Quentin Scarsbury. During the party the Rose goes missing. Scarsbury is suspected. But get this – the name of the woman *with* Lord Scarsbury that night was Adler. Miss Adler.'

'Wow!' said Billy.

'Hector's mystery woman!' cried Edie.

'She's definitely the fam we've got to shershay then!' said Potts. 'At last we got sumfing solid to go on!'

Sam told them – in spite of Potts's continuing objections – there were *three* things to be done before they could 'shershay': he wanted one of the team to visit the diamond vaults to find out who had deposited the Rose at the African Diamond Company – 'That might be one for you, Billy. Second: I must do some more research here – going through Mr Holmes's files to see if I can trace any of the names.' Lastly and most importantly, Sam explained, he wanted to visit Uncle Hector, accompanied by Potts and Dr Watson.

Potts was concerned. 'It won't get you nowhere, Sam.'

'Potts,' said Sam. 'You once told me that most card players are no good at bluffing.'

'Yeah. They twitch or do sumfing which gives them away. It's called a "tell".'

'Well, I've got a couple of questions I want to put to Hector. I want to look for his "tell".'

''Ector won't say nuffing new.'

'I don't expect him to. Don't worry, Potts. We're getting there.'

'I 'ope so.'

'We'll get Hector off. We will. But there's not much more we can do tonight, is there? I know it's boring, but we can't act without more to go on.'

Potts was forced to agree. 'I've 'eard Mr 'Olmes say that detectin' is just drudgery and detail.'

They all felt frustrated, but resigned, and agreed to meet up again later next day after the vist to Hector.

When the others had gone, Sam began combing through Holmes's files. As he did so, Titch talked to Dr Watson, who agreed – the boat was overpriced.

'But keep looking, Titch.' Echoing Sam, he added, 'Something will turn up.'

It was late as Titch and Sam made their way back to Marylebone.

'Tell you what, Titch. There's something about the evidence that narks me. You know the pearl-handled pistol that was found on the body of the Shift Manager . . .

'It's odd, ain't it? Why would the killer leave the murder weapon behind?'

'Exactly. Well, I've been thinking.'

Titch grinned. 'That's not like you.'

Sam smiled but went on intensely. 'If there was only Hector and Miss Adler in the vaults at the time of the shooting, surely one of them would have noticed the pistol.'

'Ay . . . d'you think there was someone else there, then? A third person?'

'Yeah. If there were three people there, I can imagine them arguing about the Rose, or being distracted in some way and forgetting the pistol. Yes?'

'Ay. If that's the case, then, it's not just Miss Adler we're looking for, is it?'

'No. I think she had an accomplice.'

'It's tricky this case, ain't it?'

'Yeah. It's not going to be easy finding Miss Adler, either. But we've got to crack it, Titch.'

'Ay. Poor old Potts is desperate.'

'I know. He doesn't show it much, but he is. He's desperate.'


Early the next morning, Watson organised a visit to Pentonville Prison. It reminded Sam of the workhouse where he had lived with his mother – big solid walls like a castle, and few windows. If Sam hadn't *known* it was a prison, housing a gallows, from outside it might have appeared a reassuring place, but inside, the atmosphere was dark and disturbing. Watson waited at the front desk with Sam and Potts until Inspector Lestrade appeared.

'This is most decent of you, Inspector,' said Watson. 'I really do appreciate your help.'

'Anything to oblige, Dr Watson,' said Lestrade. 'They've gone to fetch Mr Hector, by the way.' Lestrade led them down a dingy corridor. Every door had three or four locks on it. The warders looked wary and suspicious as they clanked along, bunches of keys jangling from their belts. The prisoners in their uniforms were underfed and filthy. The whole place stank.

'Has the Shift Manager's body been examined, yet, Inspector?' Watson asked.

'Not yet. We're behind, I'm afraid.' A villainous-looking turnkey let them into a room of brick, painted grey, with a bare wooden table and four plain chairs. The only light came from a small window with bars, high up on one wall. 'The autopsy on the Shift Manager is immaterial though,' Lestrade continued, 'because Hector Potts has confessed to his murder.'

Sam interrupted. 'Excuse me, sir. Is there any evidence we could *see*?'

Lestrade looked hard at Sam. 'Until we've done the

autopsy, young man, the *only* evidence is the pistol. Nasty little thing.'

'It had a pearl handle, didn't it, Inspector?'

'What a clever young gentleman you are.' Lestrade was irked by Sam's knowledge of the case. 'Here's something that perhaps you *don't* know. Inscribed on the pearl are the initials I.A. What does that tell us? I'm keen to have your view.'

'I.A?' Sam asked.

'What a memory!' said Lestrade.

Sam was unaffected by Lestade's sarcasm – he was thinking about the initials on the pistol.

'I must go,' said Lestrade. 'We've got rather a lot on.' Indicating the turnkey, he added, 'This gentleman here will take care of you.' He turned to leave.

'Looking for the Rose?' asked Sam cheekily.

Lestrade didn't like being questioned by this impertinent urchin. He looked down at Sam. 'Let me warn you, son. A little knowledge is a dangerous thing. And to answer your question – no – searching for the Rose would be a complete waste of time. It's probably out of the country. If it isn't, it'll be buried so deep on the black market, that most *villains* won't know where to find it.' He turned to the door, but Sam had really got under his skin, and he rounded on him. 'You want to watch yourself, young man. You're only here because I've asked, special-like. Dr Watson, that young lad looks like he might get above himself. Keep an eye on him. Goodbye.'

Lestrade stomped off in an ill humour as Hector arrived between two warders. His uniform was too large, and he was handcuffed. His fingers were raw, black and bleeding. Unshaven, pale and exhausted, he seemed to Potts to have shrunk in the two days since his arrest. He was pushed into one of the chairs, and the two warders who had brought him left, slamming the door behind them; the evil-looking turnkey locked it, and stood on guard in front of it.

Potts had a lump in his throat. "'Allo, Uncle. 'Ow you doin'?" he asked.

'I'm surviving, thank you. Bless you all for coming.' Hector spoke with simple sincerity. He had much less of a cockney accent than Potts or his dad – compared to them, he sounded almost refined. Sam's impression, beneath this damaged scarecrow of a figure, was of a gentle man.

'Wot's the matter wiv your 'ands?' Potts enquired.

'I've been picking oakum, Eli.'

Potts didn't like being called Eli, but under the

circumstances, he bit his tongue. 'Wot's oakum, Uncle H?'

'Old ropes full of tar; we have to unravel them so they can be reused. But the tar's sticky, and the ropes are all tangled and very sharp – it's quite tough on the fingers.' He tried to conceal his injured, handcuffed hands beneath the table.

Potts was near tears. Sam was in shock. Watson looked on aghast. To see Hector in this broken condition would have touched the hardest of hearts, let alone the tender heart of Dr John Watson.

'I've brought some friends to see you, Uncle. This is my pal, Sam, and this is Dr Watson, wot you've 'eard me speak of.'

'I know who he is, Eli. It's kind of you to have brought them – and nice of you both to come – but it's no good, you know. Not even Dr Watson's famous friend could get me off these charges. I'm guilty.' Hector was mumbling. 'Sit down and talk to me. This is a lonely place.'

The three visitors seated themselves around the prisoner at the table. Sam made sure he sat facing Hector so that he could watch him closely. Watson bent forward and carefully took Hector's handcuffed hands.

'Let me clean these up for you, Hector – may I call you Hector?'

'Please. I feel right honoured that you've come to see me. Eli talks about you all the time. And Mr Holmes of course.'

Watson took some cotton wool and a bottle of spirit from his bag and began cleaning Hector's swollen, damaged fingers, removing some of the sharper, more stubborn rope fibres stuck in his skin. To Potts it looked excruciating, but Hector made no sound – he watched as Watson worked, and smiled at the Doctor, who talked sympathetically to him. 'We are so very sorry for your trouble, Hector.'

'Thank you.'

'No one who knows you can believe this has happened, you know.' Hector looked askance at the Doctor: Sam was watching him like a hawk. 'In fact, Hector, the truth is that there is no one who knows you who believes you did it.' For a moment, Hector did not respond at all. Then he stuck his bottom lip out and tilted his head as if to say there was nothing he could do about that. 'What was Hector doing with a gun?' Watson enquired. 'That's what people are asking.'

Hector mumbled something half audible about the gun having been his for a long time, but he seemed annoyed, angry. As Watson gently cleaned Hector's fingers he asked where Hector had got the gun from. Hector's reply was still suppressed, muttered – he claimed to have had it for so long he could not remember – but again he appeared uncharacteristically irritated.

'Can *I* ask a question, please, Doctor?' asked Sam.

Watson looked to Hector. 'It's a waste of time,' Hector protested loudly. 'I did it.'

'Yes, I know that, sir,' said Sam. 'I wanted to ask about the Shift Manager.' Hector went back to watching Watson working on his hand. 'Had you worked with him for long?'

'Ten years. All the time I was at the African Diamond Company.'

'You knew him well, then?'

Hector looked distressed. 'He was my friend.'

After a nervous silence, Sam said, 'I'm sorry to ask, sir, but I don't understand *why* you shot him?'

Hector looked hard at Sam. He didn't speak. He couldn't. He was too upset. After a moment, he said, 'I feel terrible about his wife and children.' Sam noted that Hector avoided the question, and could see he was telling the truth.

'This looks a lot better now,' said Watson. 'I'll put

some balm on, if I may.' Hector almost moaned with relief as Watson applied the soothing lotion to his throbbing hand. 'How does that feel?'

'A lot easier, thank you, Doctor.'

Watson began work on Hector's other hand.

Sam shot a warning look at Potts, and asked, 'What happened to the Rose, Mr Potts?'

Hector was taken aback. He stiffened. 'What do you mean?'

'The Rose. It wasn't in the vaults. Who took it?'

'No one.'

'What do you mean, no one?'

'It wasn't there!' said Hector forcefully, taking his hand away from Dr Watson. The chains on his handcuffs clanked loudly. 'I keep telling them. *No one* took it! It wasn't there! They won't believe me!'

'Calm down, Hector. Give me your hand,' said Watson. 'Sam, don't annoy Mr Potts.'

Reluctantly, Hector gave Watson back his hand.

'Sorry, Doctor. I keep telling them the Rose wasn't in the vaults,' Hector apologised. 'The deposit box was empty. But they don't listen. I did *not* do the robbery. There wasn't one to do – the Rose was *not there*! That's the irony. This blasted tragedy need never have happened. I simply lost my head. I did the murder, but I was on my own. I had no accomplice. The police are barking up the wrong tree.'

Hector's story made no sense at all and they all felt that he was protesting rather too much.

'I don't think the police *are* barking up the wrong tree,' said Sam. 'They're on to her.'

Hector jumped up from his chair. 'Her?' he yelled, looking panicky. 'It's not what you think,' he cried, flustered and enraged.

'Leave Hector alone, Sam, and let me finish his hand.'

'Sorry,' said Sam. 'Sorry, Mr Hector. I thought they would have told you.'

'What are you talking about?' Hector demanded angrily.

'I mean about Irene Adler,' said Sam. It was as though he had lit a fuse.

'Get out!' cried Hector furiously. 'Get out and leave me alone. It wasn't *her*. She wasn't there. It had nothing to *do* with her! You can stay, Doctor, if you would, and finish my hands for me – it's helping the pain. But you!' He pointed at Sam, his handcuffs jangling violently. 'Get out!'

'Wiggins,' said Watson sharply, 'wait for me outside.' He turned to the ugly-looking turnkey, 'Officer, would you mind letting these two boys out, please? Wait for me at the front desk. Both of you. Unless you wish to stay, Potts. Do you?'

'No fanks, Doctor. I'll go wiv Sam. Goodbye, Uncle 'Ector. I'll come and see you again soon, all right?'

'Thank you, Eli. Come here.' Potts went over to his uncle. 'You're a good lad, Eli. I don't have a son of my own. I've always thought of you as my son – you've always behaved like one.' He leaned close to Potts and spoke quietly. 'And I love you like a son.' The men in Potts's family were not openly affectionate with each other, but Potts put his arms round Hector, and had to fight hard to stop himself sobbing. 'You've still got my old bowler, I see, Eli. God bless you. Come again. And bring the Doctor, if he doesn't mind tagging along. But don't bring *him*.' He nodded darkly in Sam's direction. 'Promise me that. Just don't bring him. Off you go. Go on. I'll be all right.'

Without a word, Potts let go of Hector and ran out of the room as fast as he could.

It was late morning by the time Watson joined Sam and Potts, and hailed a cab. The quiet in the cab was unbroken, even by Potts, who sat disconsolately in the corner, sniffing. Watson maintained a stony silence, throughout the journey, glaring out of the window. On the way back to Baker Street they dropped Potts off in Soho.

On arrival at 221b, Watson stalked upstairs with the curt command, 'Follow me,' directed at Sam. In the study, he ordered Sam to sit down and stood, looking like thunder, with his back to the fire. Sam had never before seen him angry.

'What on earth were you playing at, Wiggins? I arranged that visit especially, and the aim of it was not to insult Inspector Lestrade and upset Uncle Hector.'

'Sorry, sir,' said Sam. 'I am trying to get him off.'

'Well, you went a very odd way about it.'

'It's quite simple really, sir. The theory we're working on—'

'You are NOT a detective, Wiggins. How many times must I tell you?'

'No, Doctor. I'm sorry. I do get a bit carried away.'

'Carried away? I'll say!' Watson let out a great sigh, and began pacing round the room. 'I have always been worried that you would become too involved in your work for Mr Holmes. And when you mention the name of . . .' he hesitated, 'Irene Adler . . . I worry greatly. Mr Holmes thought her the only woman he had ever met capable of cold-blooded murder. He refers to her as *"the"* woman – she is the one person – apart from Professor Moriarty – ever to get the better of him. What in heaven makes you think she is involved with *Uncle Hector*? I'm sorry to be so cross with you, but after your experiences with Colonel Maltravers, you should know how dangerous people can be.' Watson was less irate now. His pacing slowed, and he took his usual armchair by the fire. 'All right. Tell me your blessed theory. Like you, I would do anything to save poor Hector from the hangman's noose.'

Sam felt that now Watson had let off steam he would be more reasonable, and he began calmly and deliberately to explain his thinking. 'Yesterday afternoon, at the newspaper library, I looked up the theft of the Rose. On the night it disappeared, the woman with the main suspect was Irene Adler.' Watson's jaw dropped. 'When I checked through the names in Mr Holmes's case files, not only did I find her *name*, I found her photograph. She's a very beautiful woman – well, you know, sir, you've met her.'

'How do you know that, Wiggins?'

'In the files, I found a reference to one of your stories – "Scandal in Bohemia" – which she's in! So I read it. A real page-turner!'

'Don't think you can get round me like that, Wiggins!'

'No, Doctor.' Sam resumed his story briskly. 'According to Hector's closest friend, Alf Jenx, Irene Adler was manipulating Hector. And when Inspector Lestrade said that the initials on the pearl-handled pistol found on the body were I.A., it seemed to me clear-cut evidence that she's involved.' Watson was now listening intently. 'Hector, of course, denied it, but his story makes no sense. He was lying.'

'Wiggins, you cannot *know* Hector was lying.'

'I watched him real close when you were doing his hands, and it was dead obvious. He couldn't tell a lie to save his life.' Watson gave Sam a wry look. 'Sorry, sir. Slightly unfortunate choice of words, like.'

'The irony is, Wiggins, that I fear you are right – he *is* telling a lie. And it *will* cost him his life.'

'And you saw what happened when I said her name. Hector went nuts.' Watson could not deny this. 'I don't believe Hector shot the Shift Manager, Doctor. I think Irene Adler – or an accomplice perhaps – might have done. And I'm pretty convinced that she, or perhaps this accomplice, has got the Rose now – how else did it *disappear*? It's nonsense Hector pretending it wasn't there. Someone took it. If I'm right, and Hector's mystery woman is Irene Adler, Hector's friend Alf would only have to take one look at Mr Holmes's photograph to confirm her identity. Inspector Lestrade would then know who to look for. And we would be a step nearer getting Hector out of that foul place. That's all, Doctor. Sorry.'

Watson sat for a few moments. 'Blast you, Sam Wiggins. Blast you, you are right.' He then looked at his half-hunter. 'Oh my goodness! Lunch-time. I must get to my surgery. It will be pandemonium. The sooner you get that photograph of . . . *"the"* woman . . .' – Watson again seemed unwilling to utter her name – 'to – what's-his-name – Alf – Alf the sooner we shall know if we can help Hector.'

Sam was relieved. Watson was his old self again. 'Thank you, sir, I'll get it done.'

'But be careful, Sam. Irene Adler,' he articulated her name with distaste, '– if it *is* her – is a very dangerous woman.'

# 4

# THE SHAMROCK

Titch was dispatched immediately to Southwalk to find Hector's friend, Alf Jenx. The very thought of Irene Adler disturbed her. Titch kept taking the photograph out of her pocket and staring into the deep-set eyes. Sam was right – Irene Adler was a remarkably beautiful woman.

When Billy returned to 221b from the African Diamond Company, where he discovered that the depositor of the Rose had been Lord Quentin Scarsbury – the man suspected of stealing it from the Astons – Sam took him round to Marylebone Station to find Edie.

'Listen, Edie. Can you spare a bit of time?'

'Now, Sam?'

'Yes.'

'I'm not doing so well today. Potts isn't here.'

'I'm free now, too, Edie,' said Billy.

'Is it important, Sam?'

'It might be, Edie. I really think we're getting somewhere, although it's been a rough morning.'

'All right. As long as I'm back for rush hour.'

'You'll have a chance to sell where we're going, Edie. Come on.'

Sam took Edie and Billy across towards Hatton Garden. On the way, he told them what had happened up at Pentonville, and explained why he needed them now. That morning, Lestrade had said the Rose would be on the black market. The Shamrock – the pub that according to the old jeweller, Ruben Curtis, was full of criminals – had stuck in Sam's mind: he wanted Edie to go in under cover of selling her herbs, and use her exceptional hearing to pick up any word, any hint, any clue as to the whereabouts of the stolen diamond. The landlord of The Shamrock wasn't too happy with under-age customers in his pub, but Edie charmed him, saying she would be working, so it didn't count, and he promised to turn a blind eye.

The Shamrock looked filthy from the outside, but when Billy took Edie into the bar, they were quite surprised. The ceilings were low and there wasn't much light. Cigarette and pipe smoke hung thick in the air, but the place was well cared for. The wooden bar was highly polished and the tables were clean. The sawdust on the floor was fresh, the brass gleamed and the spittoons had been emptied after lunch. In spite of the crush, the level of conversation was low. Billy looked round: small groups of customers were chatting secretively. Perhaps, Billy thought, they didn't want to be overheard.

Everyone fell for Edie with her auburn hair and lilting Irish brogue – after all, the pub was called The Shamrock, and quite a few of the customers were Irish. They hadn't had a pretty young flower-girl in there before, and the novelty helped her to sell her herbs easily. People bought more to drink, so the landlord was happy to let her stay.

Sam waited outside. When he was working for Mr Holmes, he was always given some kind of cover. On this occasion he had his shoeshine gear with him; setting up on the corner of Leather Lane and Hatton Garden, he managed to earn a few bob into the bargain. He had told Titch where he would be, and after a couple of hours she joined him with good news. Hector's friend, Alf Jenx, had taken one look at the photograph of Irene Adler, and said immediately, 'That's her, all right. That's Hector's mystery woman. You would never forget *her* face.' So even if Edie didn't come up with anything from the pub, the Irregulars had something definite to go on.

'Inspector Lestrade won't like this, will he?' said Titch with a grin.

'No, but he might try to find her now.'

'I wouldn't put money on it, Sam.' Titch remarked grimly.

'We'd best get her photograph to him, hadn't we?'

'Shall I take it over to Scotland Yard now?'

'That'd be great, Titch. Then come back here. I'll wait for you.'

'I'll nip down the Embankment. Jump on the back of a cab. See ya!' As Titch set off towards the river, Billy popped out of the pub to report that when someone had produced the lunch-time newspaper, the headlines were still about the murder of the Shift Manager at the African Diamond Company, and there had been some talk of the missing Rose.

'What exactly?'

'Edie said it wasn't so much about the jewel, as about some man, one of the regulars. If *he* was here, they said, *he'd* know where it was. It was a joke. He's some local character they take the mick out of. Know what I mean?'

'Has he got a name?'

'Old Jarvis, or Charvis. Something like that, she thought.'

'And . . . ?'

'He usually comes in twice a day.'

At least they hadn't drawn a complete blank. They decided their best bet was to wait, in the hope that Old Charvis turned up. Sam thought that as they now knew who to look out for, Edie could leave if she wanted to, but Billy pointed out that she was selling well and that prices were better than at Marylebone Station. 'There's some money in there, Sam, although you wouldn't think so at first.'

'High-class villains perhaps.'

'Maybe.'

'Is Edie safe in there, Billy? No hassle?'

'No. They look like a right queer lot, but they're quite nice underneath. But, Sam, I ought to get back to Baker Street if it's all the same to you.'

'You get off, Billy. We don't want to upset the Doc again. You couldn't nip in and see Potts on the way, could you? He was real down this morning.'

'I'll drop by. But he'll be running late today. There's

another big fight on down in Blackfriars.'

'Titch and me are worried about him, Billy.'

'He'll be all right, Sam. Tough as old boots is Potty!'

'If you see him, tell him to drop by 221b tomorrow morning. We'll see if we can't get things moving at last – locate Irene Adler.'

'Wow! Great! See you later maybe.'

'If there's anything worth reporting,' said Sam. 'If not, it'll be in the morning.'

Billy ran off up Leather Lane.

When he dropped in at The Silken Garter in Soho, Potts's mum – Lily – said she had never seen Potts so low as when he'd got back from Pentonville that morning. He was still out running for Mr Dyke now, just as Billy had predicted, so he left a message and hotfooted it to Baker Street, buying Watson's evening paper en route. He could find nothing about the Rose on the front page. Inside there was one insignificant paragraph which contained nothing new. To his relief, he was back before Watson returned from the surgery.

By the time Potts returned home after paying out for Mr Dyke, he was exhausted. He wasn't tired from work – he never tired – he was drained. He couldn't get the terrible images of Uncle Hector out of his mind, and the smell of the prison seemed to cling to his clothes. His mum, Lily, was playing the piano in the bar. As she finished her song, there was loud applause, and calls for more.

'In a minute, lads. Give me a break!' she called. ''Allo, my darlin' boy.' She gave Potts a big hug and a kiss. She relayed Billy's message, and asked, 'What you going to do, love?'

'Dunno, Ma. 'Ave a nap and see 'ow I feel.'

'Let me know if you're going out again.'

'Will do. You all right, Ma?'

'I'll survive, love.'

'Give us another song, Lil!'

'Comin' up, lads!' Winking at Potts as he left the bar, she launched into 'The Beaux Gendarmes'. The regulars liked this one, it gave them a chance to poke fun at Mr Potts – reformed 'gendarme'.

'*Beau* gendarme? *Bent*, more bloomin' likely!' they jeered.

Mr Potts took it well, and even joined in. Potts waved to his dad, who was leading the chorus, and, down-hearted, he crept up to his room. He didn't know how his mum and dad managed to put on such brave faces.

\* \* \*

When Edie emerged from The Shamrock, she was surprised to see Titch, who had long been back from Scotland Yard, where she had left Irere Adler's photo for Inspector Lestrade.

'Hi, Titch! Good to see ya!' Edie called. 'Sure, Sam, I'm coming here again. I did real well today. Even without Potts.'

As evening closed in, a light fog began to form. The three of them huddled together for warmth, and waited.

'We really need to stay *in* there in case this Old Charvis bloke turns up,' said Sam.

'I'll go back,' said Edie. 'They know me now. I'll ask the landlord for a glass of milk.' She left her basket with them, and went back into the pub. It was still very busy, and with the lamps lit it was warm and welcoming. Edie moved slowly among the customers. The talk was still low – intense and contained – and Edie took as long as possible to get her glass of milk. Taking her time drinking it, she stood at the bar listening hard, then thanked the landlord, who had kindly let her have it for nothing, and said goodbye. There was some talk of Old Charvis, but no sign of him.

At the door, Edie nearly bumped into a tall, thin

man, wearing a tall, thin hat. In spite of his tattered demeanour, he had an air of faded class about him. Elegantly avoiding collision with Edie, he removed his hat, held it to his chest, and made a small bow. 'My dearest young lady, I *do* apologise. Pray, forgive me.'

Edie flashed him a winning smile, gave a quick curtsy and turned to leave. As she did so, she heard several people in the bar say, 'Here he is!'

Voices called out, 'Charvis, me old mucker!'

He was obviously much liked, and was greeted with great warmth and joviality.

'We've been waitin' for ya.'

'Where ya bin, Charvy?'

'Never you mind where I have been, dear friends.' The tall thin man spoke with a wry smile, and an air of mock gentility. 'In company well above your humble station, I need hardly say.'

'Steady on!'

'Careful!'

'Buck House again, Charvy?'

'How did you know? Regrettably, I was informed by a palace flunky that Her Majesty was out.'

This was greeted with amused laughter. 'She don't *go* out these days, Charvy!'

'My belief, although it pains me to inform you,

dear listeners, is that when she heard that I was at the gates, our beloved Queen Vic, for the first time in years, vacated the palace.'

They all roared with laughter. 'What'll you 'ave, Charvy?'

'I would like a large glass of your finest porter if you please, landlord. Thank you. A beneficent offer, gratefully accepted.'

Edie ran to Sam and Titch. 'Did you see that old feller who just went in?'

'The one with the tall hat?'

'Him. It's him. He's the one we've been waiting for. What shall we do?'

'I'm thinking.' They both knew Sam well enough to leave him alone for a moment. 'Got it. We'll stay out here till he leaves. And when he does . . . this is the plan.'

Outside The Shamrock, Sam, Titch and Edie waited in the mist and dark for Old Charvis to emerge. They were getting cold, and beginning to lose heart, when they heard a familiar voice.

''Allo, you lot!'

'Potts!' Edie was particularly pleased to see him.

'Great to see you!' cried Titch.

'You all right?' enquired Sam.

'Well, I'm 'ere, ain't I?' said Potts, chuffed by the warmth of his welcome. They told him that Irene Adler had been identified from the photograph, which was already with Inspector Lestrade. They explained that Old Charvis might be another lead, and filled him in on Sam's plan.

It was late when Old Charvis tottered through the pub door. People had been plying him with drink and he was slightly the worse for wear. He bumped into the door jamb, missed one of the steps and, having arrived uncertainly on the pavement, appeared unsure which way to turn for home. Eventually he held up a knowing finger and moved off down Leather Lane.

He staggered round the bend, holding on to the wall, and stopped to draw breath. He was out of sight of the pub now, and still some way from the brighter lights of Hatton Garden; this is where Titch and Potts struck. They approached menacingly, jostled the old boy, and demanded money. Slightly inebriated, he was incapable of defending himself and was about to give them the few coins in his pocket when Sam and Edie tore up, shouting. They made a great show of frightening Potts and Titch off, and while Sam pretended to chase them away, Edie comforted Old Charvis. Potts and Titch ran off home, and by the time Sam joined Edie, she was firm friends with the old boy, who was full of gratitude, and readily accepted their offer to help him home.

''Tis but a stone's throw to Cripplegate Square, hard by Farringdon Station, and 'twill earn you an old man's undyin' gratitude.'

As they progressed slowly through the light fog, Sam had a chance to observe the old boy. His long thin nose – in keeping with his long thin hat and long thin body – was several shades redder than it should have been. His eyes were heavily lidded, above high cheekbones adorned with tufts of grey whiskers. His chin, like most things about him, was long and thin. His black suit was carefully preserved although the trousers had shrunk, and came to an end inches above his long thin feet. His ancient, well-polished, black leather shoes turned up a little towards the toe. Overall, he had the air of an emaciated Mr Punch.

Sam and Edie supported him on either side, to prevent him from wandering into the road. Carefully, they steered him back home – the old boy chattering all the way – to the dark, cramped squalor of Cripplegate Square, which turned out to be a gloomy quadrangle with rooming-houses on all four sides.

Up endless flights of uncarpeted stairs they helped

him. There were few people about at this hour: a drunken tramp snoring loudly in the stairwell, a couple of dubious-looking ladies, and a brute of a man with a vile dog who growled at them. Finally they reached a ladder, leading to Charvis's poky garret. He asked them to join him in his 'humble and impecunious abode'. Up the rickety ladder, and into his attic room under the bare beams, they went.

The cold walk had sobered him up a little. Sam and Edie settled him in the chair – the only other pieces of furniture were a small chest of drawers and a bed poking out from under the eaves. While Edie rooted about to see if she could make him a drink, Sam steered the conversation round to diamonds; he was keen to get on to the subject of the Rose. Old Charvis told them that diamonds had been the love of his life – a life ruined, he claimed, by one foolish, illegal transaction. He had lost everything, and spent time in prison. He sighed repeatedly. 'What a fool I was. What a fool. Lost everything – home, family, future! But now, my dear children – how kind you have been to me – I am back! I am back and on the edge. Right on the edge.'

'What do you mean, Mr Charvis, sir?' asked Sam.

'On the edge of a comeback,' replied Old Charvis, placing a long, thin, knuckly finger on the side of his nose and giving Sam a knowing look. 'Thanks to the lady I am workin' for now, a mighty gem is goin' to change my dismal fortunes, and shine a ray of light on my declinin' years!' Edie heard this and stopped stirring the sweet-smelling brew she was heating up on the small stove, which she had coaxed into life. She caught Sam's eye. They wondered who Old Charvis's lady might be. His long thin finger delved into his waistcoat pocket. 'Just for fun,' he said, and took out a small felt envelope. From it, like a conjuror producing a rabbit out of a hat, he produced a jewel – a large pink diamond.

'Phew!' gasped Edie, thinking for a minute that they might have stumbled on the Rose.

'Incredible!' gasped Sam. 'May I see?'

Old Charvis gave Sam the jewel. He held it to the light. Turned it. Examined it. Then he remembered Ruben's simple test – a diamond held to the lips is cold. Glass is warmer.

'This is not real!' he cried.

Old Charvis was rather disappointed. 'Ah, Sam. You are a clever boy. It's glass, but it fools some people!' Sam handed the fake back to Old Charvis, who smiled ruefully. 'Just a bit of fun.'

'I've always been intrigued by diamonds,' said Sam.

This earned him an old-fashioned look from Edie as she gave Charvis his drink.'

'Thank you, my darlin' girl. How clever of you to get that old stove workin'! It's quite warm in here now. Mmmmm. Delicious. I was just like Sam, you know,' Charvis mused, 'obsessed by diamonds. And here I am, as I say, on the edge!' He leaned forward, close to Sam, who was kneeling on the floor, and whispered, 'Very soon! Very, very soon!'

'I'm glad to hear that, sir. Do you mean you've got your hands on something big now?'

'That's right, my dear, clever Sam. Well . . . not exactly *got my hands on*. Have *access to*, to be strictly truthful. The point is that I am now in a position to restore my former fortunes. I am actually quite well born, dear children, although you could be forgiven for thinkin' otherwise.'

'A big stone, eh?'

The old man nodded. The corners of his lips turned up into a sweet, satisfied smile.

Sam went on, 'I've always wanted to see a really famous gem. Pink Sunrise. Or the Star of the South. Unbelievable.'

Edie was impressed by Sam's knowledge, and pulled a face at him as she knelt with Sam at Charvis's feet.

'Edie, my darlin' girl, I'm sorry I can't offer you a chair. Young Sam here appears to know a thing or two about diamonds, doesn't he? Let's give him a little test, shall we?' Edie nodded, slightly unsure of what she was letting Sam in for.

'What do the four C's stand for, my boy? D'you know?'

'Yes, sir. Cut. Clarity. Carat weight. And Colour.'

'Good. You mentioned the Star of the South. What do you know about it?'

'It's brownish pink, and cushion-shaped.'

'Excellent.' Charvis rubbed his hands together. 'Let's see . . . name me three other famous diamonds.' He was excited, like a boy who has found a new chum to play with.

'Well, everyone knows the Darya-i-Nur,' said Sam, 'so that doesn't count, really. There's the Hortensia. And the Steinmetz – the jewel in the crown, as they call it.' Ruben Curtis, the jeweller, would have been proud of his pupil – Sam had remembered everything! 'But the one I'd die to see is this one that's in the news right now. Pear-shaped. 125 carats, and emits a beautiful pink glow, supposedly. Yes, Mr Charvis, sir, I'd give anything to see the Rose of Africa.'

Old Charvis looked as though he had been slapped.

On the mention of the Rose, his hand shot guiltily to the waistcoat pocket in which he had put the fake, and his face changed instantly from sweet diamond enthusiast to frightened and dangerous weasel. He leaned forward and put his hand on the rug. Sam and Edie watched, confused. Suddenly he sat bolt upright, looked hard at Edie, then turned on Sam.

'Who sent you?' he spat.

Sam and Edie were both genuinely surprised by the question. 'Sent us, sir?'

'Yes.' He was startled and angry. 'Who sent you?'

In one hand he was holding the drink Edie had made for him. She took the other and stroked it gently. 'Sure, no one sent us, Mr Charvis, sir. We're just us – Sam and Edie.'

'We saw you being done over by those two hooligans and rescued you,' said Sam. 'Remember?'

Charvis was less troubled now 'For a minute I thought . . . You see,' he added confidentially, as Edie continued to stroke his hand, 'there is a great deal at stake, and the gentleman with whom I am workin' does not like me or trust me. I thought *he* might have sent you. But I see now that you are the genuine article – 100 carat! Forgive me for doubtin' you, but diamonds can be an unpleasant business. Especially when one is movin' in – how shall I say – *deep waters?*'

'Look, sir,' said Sam, 'I'm sorry I upset you, and if it's all the same to you, it's late, and time for us to go. Come on, Edie. Let's be away and leave Mr Charvis alone.' Edie was surprised by the speed with which Sam was suddenly preparing to go. He was already at the door.

'Will you be all right now then, Mr Charvis?' she asked. 'On your own, like?'

'Of course I will, my dear little Edie. My head is a great deal clearer now, thanks to your delicious beverage. Off you trot. One moment, I want to give you a little somethin' for rescuin' me.'

'We didn't do it for money, sir!' they protested – hoping that Old Charvis would insist. And he did. He gave them both a penny.

'Off you go now. Goodbye.'

They thanked him. Then Sam was out of the door and down the ladder like greased lightning, with Edie on his heels.

'To be sure, Sam, leaving that quick was a bit rude, like.'

'Don't worry, Edie, he wanted us gone.'

'What?'

'You saw him touch the floor?'

'Sure, I did. Very peculiar.'

'He'll be checking under the floorboards now. He's got something hidden under there. But best of all –' Sam was really elated, '– I know what I need to know.'

'He didn't tell us anything!'

'He did, Edie. He's involved, for definite. The fake he showed us was pear-shaped, and pink – like the rose. And you saw him when I *mentioned* the Rose! If *he* hasn't got it, the lady or the gent he's working for *have*. That fits my theory and all.'

'What theory?'

'That the woman had an accomplice. All we have to do is watch him, and he'll take us to her.'

'Well, I surely hope you're right, Sam, but I don't think it'll be that easy meself.'

'Let's get you home, Edie. And tomorrow morning, if Potts'll give me odds, I'll bet good money that in the next couple of days we shall set our eyes on the current owner of the Rose of Africa.'

'D'you mean Miss Adler?'

'That's exactly who I mean, Edie. Miss Irene Adler.'

# 5

# ON OUR OWN

The Irregulars took it in turns to stake out Old Charvis. They watched every move he made, which wasn't difficult. He went to The Shamrock at lunch-time and in the evenings. He spent most of one afternoon with a glass-blower whose small works were discreetly situated underneath the railway arches in Kentish Town. He went twice to Fox Court, rooming-houses off the Gray's Inn Road. On one occasion he left there with a smart-looking man. Titch and Potts were on duty at that time; they tailed Charvis and his well-dressed friend to a wine lodge near King's Cross Station. But after three days, Sam's confident prediction that they would set eyes on Irene Adler, whom he believed to be in possession of the Rose, had come to nothing.

As the time for Uncle Hector to appear at the Old Bailey drew nearer, Potts was not his usual larky self at all, which upset Edie. Billy tried to keep their spirits up, but he, too, was losing faith in what they were doing. Titch was worried about Sam, who was demonic – baffled, and angry with himself, pacing up and down, reviewing the facts, trying to work out where he had gone wrong.

At the end of the third fruitless day, they held an emergency council back at Baker Street. Mrs Hudson retired to her room, leaving them the run of her kitchen. At Sam's insistence they went over and over the facts.

'We know Irene Adler is Hector's mystery woman. Right?'

They all agreed without any real enthusiasm.

'And we're pretty sure Old Charvis is involved.' This brought no response from the Irregulars. 'Come on, you lot! Help me out.'

'All right,' said Billy.

'Why would Old Charvis go to a glass-blower?'

'Because he deals in fake jewellery,' said Edie.

Sam agreed. 'But he hasn't been *back* there, has he?' He hadn't. 'Let's run through the King's Cross trip again.'

'Not again, Sam!' Potts and Titch protested.

'We have to,' insisted Sam. 'We *must* find Irene Adler – Lestrade's not bothering – and it's all we've got to go on.'

So once again they ran through Old Charvis's outing to the King's Cross wine lodge.

'Now concentrate. All of you,' Sam urged. 'There's a clue in this somewhere. We *have* to spot it.'

Titch kicked off. 'Charvis picks up his smart mate from Fox Court.'

'How old do you reckon his mate is?' Sam asked.

'About thirty-five.'

'Wears a fick overcoat 'n' a topper. Carries a cane,' added Potts.

'*Very* well dressed.'

'Got a fin moustache.'

'What do you two *make* of this friend of Charvis's?' Edie enquired.

'Posh. Gentlemanlike.'

'Nice manners, sort of fing. 'Olds the door open for the old boy.'

'Far too smart for a dump like Fox Court,' observed Titch.

'That's an interestin' point, Titch,' said Potts.

'Very,' said Sam. 'Could be important. So . . .

together, Charvis and Posh Friend head off towards King's Cross. Right?'

'Right.'

Titch continued. 'On the way to King's Cross they are joined by someone else.'

'Can you describe him?' Sam demanded.

'Bloke in a black cape.'

'Black cape. Height?'

'Very tall. Taller than Old Charvis.'

'Top 'at 'n' all. Looked like a bloomin' great black bird.'

'Age?'

'Early twennies, Titch, d'you reckon?' said Potts.

'Ay. Early twenties.'

Sam summarised. 'So . . . we've got three of them – Old Charvis – tall and thin.'

'The Blackbird. Even taller!'

'And Posh Friend from Fox Court.'

'Good. These three go to a wine lodge near King's Cross. Yes?'

'Yes,' chorused Titch and Potts.

'In the wine lodge, they meet two men – what are *they* like?'

'One was a policeman,' said Titch.

'The other,' added Potts, 'was a real nasty-looking

geezer. Reminded me of that officer guardin' the door when we was wiv 'Ector up in the prison.'

Sam considered this for a moment. 'These two men – let's call them the Policeman and the Officer – did they *give* Charvis anything?'

'No,' said Titch.

Sam was baffled. 'Now concentrate. Hard. This is where something odd happens. Charvis, Posh Friend and the Blackbird do not receive *anything* from their two contacts. You're absolutely sure?'

'Ay.' Titch was adamant. 'But Charvis's Posh Friend . . .'

'From Fox Court?'

'Ay. He gave *the Officer* an envelope.'

'An envelope.' Sam paced, muttering, 'It's this envelope that's key. I'm sure.' He shook his head. 'Which way did they go when they left the wine lodge?'

'Who?'

'The Policeman and the Officer.'

'Dunno. Titch and me was followin' Old Charvis and 'is pals.'

'Charvis just went back home. Posh and Blackbird took a cab.'

'So where did their two contacts in the wine lodge go? With an envelope.'

'The Policeman went down towards King's Cross, didn't 'e, Titch?'

'That direction. And the Officer – who had received the envelope from Charvis's posh chum – he went up towards the Angel, maybe back to Pentonville.'

Sam paced on, still shaking his head. He wanted them to go over it all again, but Potts couldn't take any more, and blurted out, 'We're gettin' nowhere, Sam. I just wanna find Irene flippin' Adler, and all we do is keep goin' over the same ol' stuff!'

'We can't find her because we're missing something, Potts. Think what Mr Holmes says – *It's there. I just can't see it.* But all right, let's take a break and look at the other thing: Titch said you might have been followed. When exactly?'

'Up near King's Cross,' said Titch. 'I had this feeling there were someone behind us.'

Edie pressed the question harder. 'Was it just a *feeling* you were being followed?'

'Potts actually *saw* someone, didn't you, Potts?'

'Describe him,' Sam demanded.

''E was squat. Burly. Black side whiskers. Huge moustache, all over his mouth. Creepy.'

'Great black boots but trying not to be noticed,' Titch prompted.

'That's right. Creepin' along, clingin' to the wall. I only caught sight of 'im a couple of times. I tried to point 'im out to Titch, but 'e kept disappearin'.'

Sam was still pacing round the kitchen table, thinking.

'*You* never saw him, Titch?' Billy enquired.

'No. Just Potts.'

It was Potts who noticed a distant look on Edie's face. 'You all right, luv?'

'Sure. I'm just getting this picture.'

Sam stopped pacing and listened.

'Wot is it, Edie?'

'I don't like to say.'

'Wot?'

'It's Uncle Hector. I don't think he's very well.'

Sam turned from Edie to Potts 'Where did you say the Officer went when he left the wine lodge?'

'You shouldn't ignore Edie, Sam!' Potts retaliated.

'I'm not.'

'When she sees sumfing like this, she's always right.'

'I know, Potts, I know. I'm thinking about it.' Sam was still now. His eyes were closed. 'The Policeman went back to King's Cross. Right?'

'Right.' Sam's fists were clenched, and he was shaking them in front of his temples, as though he was going to hit himself to get his thoughts together. 'It's there. I know it's there! Why can't I see it?' Sam cried in frustration. 'The Officer – the one who was given the envelope – the nasty-looking guy who reminded Potts of the warden at Pentonville – went up towards the Angel. Right?'

'Right.'

Suddenly, Sam went deathly white.

'What's the matter, Sam?'

'I've got it. I've got it. It's Uncle Hector.'

'What is it, Sam?'

'Edie's right. We must go and see Dr Watson immediately.'

'Wot's up?'

Sam looked at them gravely. 'I think Hector's life may be in danger.'


In the study, Watson was sitting peacefully by the fire, reading the *Royal Medical Journal*. He was researching eye disease in order to assist Edie, and was engrossed in a piece about trachoma, an infection currently raging among immigrants in New York. He was alarmed by a sudden noise – it sounded like a stampede. Before he could lay the *Journal* to one side, the door burst open and the Irregulars rushed in.

'What on earth—?'

'Please, Doctor,' pleaded Sam, 'we need to get to Pentonville as fast as possible.'

'Pentonville?'

'Fast,' said Potts.

'We think Hector's life may be in danger,' said Titch.

'Hector's life?' Watson was confused.

'Yes, Doctor. We need to get there as fast as we can to prevent—'

'Billy! Stop!' cried Watson.

'Sorry, sir, but it's VERY urgent.' Sam was beside himself.

'Calm down. Calm down all of you. Explain yourselves.'

'We haven't got *time*, sir,' said Titch

'We have to go *now*,' shouted Billy.

'We may already be too late,' said Edie.

'We need to get word to Inspector Lestrade,' added Sam.

'Hold on, hold on. You have all got completely carried away . . .'

'No, sir. I've *seen* it! It's for real,' Edie begged.

'It is, Dr Watson.' They were *all* begging.

Watson was stumped. He had great respect for Edie's visions. 'Goodness gracious, what am I to do with you?' They stood looking plaintively at the Doctor, who took his place in front of the fire, but before he could speak, Potts walked up to him.

'Please, sir, I know it's a tall order, but I reckon Edie and Sam are on to sumfing 'ere. If you're not game for this, and if it's all the same wiv you, I'm goin' to Pentonville on me tod. Cos I don't want nuffing else to 'appen to 'Ector. It's bad enough for 'im as it is.' Potts turned and, with all eyes on him, walked miserably to the study door. The sight of this normally larky character looking so bereft was too much for Watson.

'Potts,' said Watson. Potts turned and looked wanly at the Doctor. 'Do you really think Hector is in danger?' They all nodded frantically. 'Oh, very well, very well. Billy, get a telegram off to Lestrade at Scotland Yard. Ask him to meet me at Pentonville as soon as he can. And call a cab. But I warn you, if this turns out to be a wild-goose chase, I shall forbid you all to have anything more to do with Mr Holmes or any of his cases ever again.'

Watson took Potts and Sam with him in the cab. Sam tried to explain, but Watson was in no mood to listen. When they arrived at Pentonville, Inspector Lestrade was already there. He was flustered, and not at all pleased to see Sam again. Sam had really got under his skin at their last meeting. He looked darkly at Dr Watson.

'Did you get my wire, Inspector?' Watson enquired.

'No, Doctor. I've been here for hours.'

'Is something wrong?' asked Watson.

'Something *is* wrong, Doctor. Very wrong.' Potts and Sam nudged each other. 'This evening two crimes have been committed – both of them connected with the murder at the African Diamond Company.'

'Is it Uncle 'Ector?' Potts demanded.

Lestrade looked down at the vulnerable young figure before him. 'I'm afraid it is, Master Potts,' he said ominously.

'Wot? Is 'e unwell?'

'Worse than that I fear.'

'*Wot?* Is 'e all right?'

'We hope so.'

'Wot's 'appened to 'im?' Potts was beside himself with anxiety.

'Easy, lad. We got to him in time.'

'WOT'S 'APPENED?' shouted Potts. 'Tell me!'

'There has been an attempt to murder him.' Watson and Potts both looked at Sam in amazement – he had been right. Edie had been right. Lestrade continued,

'When they found Mr Hector he was on his last legs, but they whipped him over to the prison hospital, and got the stomach pump on him. Poison in his afternoon tea, we think. They expect him to recover, but there's no point you going over to see him, Master Potts – he's semi-conscious. *You* can take a look at him in a professional capacity if you wish, Dr Watson.'

'I would like that, Inspector. Thank you.'

'Poor old 'Ector,' moaned Potts.

'He will pull through, I'm sure.' Lestrade was reassuring. 'What interests me, however, is why you are all here.'

'Well,' said Watson, looking at Sam, 'Wiggins – whom I am sure you remember –' Lestrade glowered at Sam, '– feared that something like this was about to happen, so we cabled you, and came ourselves as fast as we could.'

Lestrade scowled at Sam. He didn't like clever little boys, especially when they turned out to be right.

'You said there was another crime committed this evening, sir,' said Sam boldly. 'Can you tell us what it was?'

Lestrade could gladly have wrung Sam's neck. 'Well, Detective Inspector Wiggins,' he said venomously, 'it grieves me to report that the evidence – by which I mean the pearl-handled pistol used in the murder – has been stolen from Scotland Yard.'

'Of course,' said Sam.

This was more than Lestrade could tolerate. 'Would you mind, Dr Watson, getting these young persons out of my sight?'

'No. Wait. Please,' said Sam, not allowing himself to be bullied by Lestrade. 'This is further evidence that the person behind all these crimes, Inspector – and you won't like this any more than the Doctor – is Irene Adler – the woman whose photograph Titch took to Scotland Yard for you days ago.'

'That is enough!' yelled Lestrade. 'Get this child out of here. This is a grown-up's game, sonny. Doctor, when *they* . . .' – he could barely bring himself to look at Sam and Potts – 'have left the premises, I shall arrange for you to visit Mr Hector.'

Sam was on the point of protesting, but Watson wisely persuaded him not to anger the Inspector further. As they were led towards the front desk, Watson remarked, 'I must say, Wiggins, you have the most extraordinary knack of rubbing old Lestrade up the wrong way. Rather like Mr Holmes.'

'Perhaps it's cos Sam's always right, and Lestrade is always wrong,' said Potts in Sam's defence.

Watson put his hand on Potts's shoulder. 'You may have a point, Potts. But if you take my advice, you'll keep it to yourself. Go straight back to Baker Street – the pair of you. Take a cab. And wait for me there. Here is some money. I shall do what I can for Uncle Hector, and be with you directly.' He turned back into the prison. Potts and Sam were eventually pushed out on to the street by a disinterested warder.

When they arrived at Baker Street, Billy, Titch and Edie were still there. They all sat waiting apprehensively for Dr Watson, eager for news. It was late when he returned and summoned them to the study. The atmosphere was chilly.

'First things first. Hector was poisoned, as Lestrade suspected – a simple test on what was left of his tea revealed traces of arsenic – but he will pull through.' They were all relieved, particularly Potts. 'Now. Wiggins.' Watson's tone was distinctly frosty. 'What exactly have you all been up to?'

Sam took a deep breath, and explained. Watson listened attentively. 'Well, sir, when we staked out Old Charvis, I was convinced he would take us to Irene Adler, because, like I told you, I'm certain she has the Rose – her or an accomplice. But she never appeared, and I was stumped. I didn't get it. Then it hit me. At the end of your story "Scandal in Bohemia" Miss Adler has supposedly left England. You and Mr Holmes arrive back here at Baker Street; this feller passes you in the street and says "Goodnight", and Mr Holmes doesn't realise till later that it's her – Miss Adler – disguised as a man.'

'Quite correct, Wiggins.'

'Well, that's it – she's in disguise now.'

'Cor blimey, Sam. Which one is she?'

Watson looked beadily at Sam. 'Be very careful, Wiggins.'

'Yes, sir. Remember Old Charvis went up to King's Cross with his Posh Friend from Fox Court?'

'Course I remember. It was me 'n' Titch follered 'em!'

'Well, that's her. The Posh Friend '

'I don't believe it! 'E's got a 'tache an' all!'

'Well, she's very clever – the Doctor'll vouch for that.'

Watson did not seem convinced. 'Really, Wiggins. This all seems pretty unlikely to me.'

'I'm certain it's her, Doctor. Hear me out. Old Charvis and Miss Adler go to a wine lodge with their friend who we call the Blackbird. In the wine lodge, they meet two men. Miss Adler hands over an envelope to one of them. It was money. It may also have contained arsenic. The Officer – who reminded Potts of the turnkey at Pentonville – goes to the prison and administers the arsenic to Hector. The other – the Policeman – goes to Scotland Yard where he lifts the pearl-handled pistol. It all fits, because the one person who is in danger in all this is Irene Adler. If Hector blabs, she's done for. *She's* the one with the motive. Right? And Hector's trial is imminent?'

'Well . . .'

'Her pistol – with I.A. on the handle – is found on the body. She may even have done the murder – remembering what Mr Holmes said, Doctor . . .'

'That she was the only woman he had ever met capable of cold-blooded murder. Correct again, Wiggins. Well, Lestrade is now in a position to act if he wishes.'

'He's done nothing about the photograph, has he?' Watson was lost for words. 'It's her, Doctor. Irene Adler. Lestrade could at least try and find her, and bring her in for questioning. The trouble is he refuses to believe us. He thinks we're just kids.'

All the good Doctor could say when he did speak was, 'Remarkable.' Watson looked doubtfully at the small irregular police force. 'What a team you are!' He then turned his back on them and stood gazing into the fire. After some minutes, he said, 'Run along all of you. It's late and I need to think this over. We shall talk about it first thing in the morning.'

Back in their secret room, Sam and Titch were unable to sleep.

Titch's voice came softly through the dark. 'Sam.'

'I'm thinking.'

'What about?'

'The Blackbird.'

'You mean, who he is?'

'Exactly.'

'Is it important?'

'I think he might be the third person, Titch.'

'The accomplice?' Titch thought for a moment. I tell you what, Sam. You were right about Lestrade. He isn't going to be any use at all.

'No. Titch.'

'Ay? What?'

'I've got a feeling . . .'

'What?'

'. . . that, without Mr Holmes around, Dr Watson's getting cold feet. So I reckon . . .'

'What?'

'If we're going to find Irene Adler . . .'

'Ay?'

'I reckon we're on our own.'

# 6

# PITCH AND TOSS

The Irregulars were summoned early to 221b by Dr Watson. Potts did not appear. Sam's fears were confirmed. Watson repeated that Lestrade now had all the information available, and that if he saw fit, he could act upon it. After receiving a cable from Holmes he was confident the Great Detective would be back within a few days. He instructed Sam and the team to do nothing more before Holmes's return. He made only passing mention of Irene Adler – referring to her (as Sherlock Holmes did) as '*the* woman'. Far from being put off, Sam was increasingly intrigued by her combination of beauty and dangerousness. He was even more determined to find her, in order to help Hector.

\* \* \*

In spite of feeling down, Potts turned up at Marylebone Station later to help Edie.

'I couldn't face the Doc this morning. Sorry.'

'Sure. We all knew what he was going to say.'

Although he was off colour, Potts was an instinctive salesman, and they did well. He began to feel better and quite soon Edie's herbs had all gone. By the time he walked Edie back home to the rookeries of Lisson Grove, Potts was more himself.

'How are you feeling about Hector, Potty?'

''Elpless, and I'm fed up wiv finkin' about 'it 'n' gettin' nowhere. 'Ow are *you*, Edie? 'Ow's your eyes?'

'Sure, Dr Watson is real kind to me, and I'm taking proper care now. They're no worse, I'll say that. And he says if I look after them, it'll be years before I lose my sight completely.'

'Tell you wot – if that 'appens, I'll give you one of *my* eyes.'

'Ah, get on with you.'

'No I will. We'd 'ave a pair between us, wouldn't we?'

'Don't make me laugh. Are you coming in? Or are you off to work for Mr Dyke, now?'

Potts wanted to go home and be alone. 'I gotta run,' he said evasively.

Edie sensed his discomfort. 'You won't be doing

anything else, will you? I mean . . . take care of yourself today.'

'Why? You been seein' fings?'

'I have actually.'

'Wot?'

'A body. I just see a body. Sort of upside down in a corner.'

'Uncle 'Ector?'

'It's not clear.'

'One of *us*?'

'I don't think so.'

'Who then?'

'I don't know. It might be the old boy.'

'Old Charvis?'

'Yes. Anyway, I just want you to take care of yourself.'

'I *will*,' said Potts, looking fondly into Edie's failing eyes. 'I wish you could give us a lead on Irene Adler, Edie.'

'La Belle Dame! So do I.'

He gave her a peck on the cheek. 'Bye.'

'Goodbye, Potty. Thanks for this morning.'

'See ya!' said Potts.

Edie watched him run off. He was the only boy who had ever maintained any interest in her after finding out about her eyes. She was apprehensive, and she didn't want anything to happen to him. She was too fond of him.

When Sam and Titch left Baker Street, Sam needed to be on his own.

'Meet me at The Shamrock at lunch, Titch.'

'Sam,' said Titch, 'Dr Watson . . . '

'I know, I know. I just can't let it go. It's poor old Potts. See you later.' He stalked off. Titch didn't mind. When he was preoccupied, she knew he was best left alone.

Sam was frustrated. The case kept eluding him. Apart from Old Charvis himself, the only concrete lead they had was Charvis's Posh Friend, who Sam was convinced was Irene Adler in disguise. So he set off for Fox Court, hoping to see for himself this 'gentleman' – Uncle Hector's mystery woman.

Sam was furious now that they had entrusted Lestrade with Irene Adler's photograph, and even crosser that the Inspector had done nothing with it. Her haunting face, with its high cheekbones, full lips and pleading eyes kept coming into his mind. Her hair was fair and soft, falling gently over her forehead and temples, but Sam could see it was a strong face that lent itself easily to masculine disguise. He tried to imagine her, disfigured, as he saw it, by a moustache. As he trudged down Gray's Inn Road, it began to drizzle.

The disorderly buildings crammed around Fox Court were in sore need of attention. Broken pipes led down cracked walls from ill-repaired gutterings, spilling their noisome contents into the well of the court, where half-naked children played, throwing pebbles at each other, kicking the filthy puddles as they ran. Women gossiped and rowed. From each shadowy corner of the dark central courtyard, narrow passages led outwards, giving it the feel of an underground warren. The noise and smell were overwhelming. If Sam was right, and Irene Adler was holed up in this unlikely place, he knew *why* – the police would never think of looking for a society lady here.

There were four blocks of five floors each – with people coming and going all the time, poor people. Sam began exploring the stairways. Up and down he went, wondering which of the many doors led to Irene Adler's room. He was looking for the posh figure that Potts and Titch had described – in a thick overcoat and top hat, carrying a walking cane, sporting a pencil moustache. He was on the second floor of the main building when he had the shock of his life. There she was. In front of him. Irene Adler. But she was not dressed as a man. Sam's heart stopped.

She was coming out of her room, keeping her head – which was draped in a dowdy shawl – well down. Even in the drab clothes she had chosen to conceal her identity she was strikingly lovely. Sam was magnetised by her beauty. He knew he had to act quickly, or lose his chance. He approached her. His mouth was dry.

'Excuse me, ma'am, can I please speak to you?' The woman looked down at him. Her eyes were the lightest, most lucid blue. 'In private, please, ma'am.'

'I beg your pardon, boy.' Her voice was low and gentle, full of gracefully concealed surprise and touched with a mild disdain.

'I need to talk to you in private, ma'am. I've got a message for you.'

She seemed amused. 'A message?'

'Yes, ma'am.'

'From whom?' she said, leaning down, close to Sam.

'I don't like to say here . . .'

'Don't be shy, sweet boy.' Her lips were pouting at him. 'What a sweet boy you are.' She was teasing him, playing with him. 'Who is your message from?'

Sam remembered Watson's warning – *she is a very dangerous woman* – but he was bewitched. He stood on tiptoe, cupping his hands round his mouth so that only she should see, so that only she should hear, and whispered, 'It's from Mr Hector Potts, ma'am.'

The woman drew herself up and away from Sam, and gazed at him with the remote objectivity of a cat. 'I am sorry, sweet boy, but you are addressing the wrong person. I have never heard of Hector Potts.' Sam was disarmed – it was Irene Adler beyond question. What game was she playing? 'Who is the intended recipient of this message?' she purred.

Still cupping his hands, still in a whisper, Sam replied, 'It's for you, ma'am. Miss Irene Adler.'

'Irene Adler?' repeated the woman. 'That is not *my* name, sweet boy. Nor have I ever heard it before.' She looked deep into Sam's eyes. 'Goodbye, sweet boy.' It was a charming dismissal.

Sam stared at her. Even her rejection of him was spellbinding. He saw instantly why Hector had been smitten. He could not tear his eyes away from her. She returned his gaze.

'Forgive me,' she said, breaking the deadlock. 'I have forgotten something.' She pushed open the door behind her and retreated into her room. Before shutting the door, she looked at Sam again – with the hint of a smile – and repeated, 'Goodbye, sweet boy. I hope you find your Miss . . . Adler, was it?'

The door closed. Sam was glued to the spot. It was *her*, Irene Adler, the woman from Sherlock Holmes's picture; there was not the slightest doubt in his mind. When he was able to move, Sam staggered down the stairs and collapsed against the wall in a dim corner of the court. He was shocked at the spell this woman had exerted on him – even in rejection he had found her enchanting, almost motherly. No wonder Hector had fallen for her. No wonder Sherlock Holmes called her '*the* woman'. Sam sat until he had recovered his breath. She did not emerge.

Some quarter of an hour later, Sam noticed a well-dressed man exiting the archway of the main stairwell. He disappeared into one of the passages leading from the court. It took Sam a moment, but . . . the overcoat and top hat, the walking cane and the pencil moustache. It was her – Irene Adler – in disguise. He pulled himself together and set off in pursuit, only to find himself in a maze of alleys and smaller courts. 'The man' was nowhere to be seen. Sam was stunned, so lost in admiration for her nerve and expertise, he almost forgot his appointment with Titch.

Titch was at The Shamrock ahead of him. Sam, still under Irene Adler's spell explained what had happened, and said he wanted to talk to Old Charvis, to see if he could find out more about the lady Charvis claimed to be working with. Unusually, there was no sign of him in the pub. Nor was he at home in his attic in Cripplegate Square. It was annoying, and further increased Sam's frustration.

'Every time I get hold of this case, Titch, there's nothing there. Let's go back to Fox Court. Keep an eye open for Irene Adler. I'm sure it's her!'

'Sam! Dr Watson told us not to do anything at all.'

'Titch, Lestrade's doing nothing. Hector's still in trouble. The moment he's well enough they'll whip him into court.'

'It's dangerous, Sam. Everyone keeps warning us – Lestrade, the Doc. This woman is dangerous.'

'I know. But she'll move now, to avoid detection, and it'd be fatal to lose her.'

Titch tried to argue Sam out of it, but he could not be shifted. It was as though he was in the grip of a fever. Reluctantly, Titch gave in and they set off for Fox Court. On the way, Titch told Sam she had been to see Potts.

'That was nice, Titch. How's he doing?'

'He's coping, but Edie's upset him.'

'Edie? How?'

'She's been seeing things again.'

'What?'

'A body.'

'No!'

'Ay. A dead body in a corner.'

'Who?'

'She didn't know.'

'That *is* worrying. She's always right.'

'Ay.'

'We'll just have to be dead careful, Titch.'

'I'll remind you of that when people start dying!'

'Don't be daft.'

Disturbed by Edie's vision, they walked in silence till they reached Fox Court. The rain had stopped and a small crowd had gathered to play Pitch and Toss. Titch had never seen it before. 'What is it, Sam?'

'It's a con. People place bets on the toss of a coin.'

The man calling the shots was thin and weedy, but he had a deep, rasping voice, and held the crowd rapt.

'He wins every bloomin' time, Sam! How does he do it?'

'He uses double-headed halfpennies, and palms the ones he shows the punters.'

'But he's right under their noses!'

Sam and Titch worked out that the barker was part

of a team: there were three others on the lookout, one of whom played the game if trade was slack – *he* would always win – which attracted customers. These three support men rotated their roles so that the set-up was not too obvious.

As the afternoon closed in, it began to turn cold. Once again the dusk brought fog with it – not a heavy 'London particular', but a fine, clingy mist. It had been overcast and damp all day. The evening arrived dark and moonless. The cobbles became dank and slippery. As lights flickered on in the soiled windows of the court, everything appeared ghostly. All Sam and Titch could do was wait and see if Irene Adler might appear.

To pass the time, Sam got a coin out of his pocket, and held it up between the finger and thumb of his left hand. 'Watch closely, Titch.' He then took the coin with his right hand. Fisting both hands, he held them out and asked Titch to choose which hand the coin was in. Titch touched Sam's right fist. Sam turned his right hand over: the palm was empty. 'Show me the other hand!' Titch cried. That too was empty. The coin had vanished. Titch couldn't believe it. 'How did you do that?'

'It's easy really,' said Sam. 'You *thought* I took the coin, but I didn't. While you were watching the hand you *thought* the coin was in, I slipped it up my other sleeve. If I straighten my arm out now, down by my side – like this – the coin drops into my hand. Look.' He held out the coin. Titch was amazed. 'Fun, isn't it?'

Titch was impressed. 'I didn't know you could do that.'

'Ah, Titch,' said Sam with a wry grin, 'nothing is what it seems.'

'Hey, look!'

Sam turned and saw that the crowd was dispersing. 'What's going on?'

One of the lookouts must have given a signal, because the team of con men vanished suddenly, and in seconds the crowd disappeared into the passages leading from Fox Court. When two policemen appeared, there was not a trace of the illegal proceedings. They continued on their beat, strolling through the court, leaving only a few stragglers loitering eerily in the shadows. Titch nudged Sam.

'Don't look, but there's a man over there who looks just like Potts's description of the bloke who followed us up at King's Cross yesterday.'

'The creepy squat bloke?'

'The Creeper. Ay. With a big moustache. Can't see

his mouth at all.'

Sam manoeuvred himself round so that he could see the half-hidden figure leaning against the wall, smoking. He *was* squat. He was dark. And he had a huge moustache.

'Potts's description to the letter,' said Sam. '*You* never saw him, did you?'

Titch shook her head. 'He saw me though.' Titch drew her cap down over her eyes and shrank into the corner. 'What's he doing here?'

'Same as us, perhaps. Looking for Irene Adler. Maybe he wasn't following *you* yesterday, but her.' The squat figure of the Creeper stiffened. Sam thought perhaps he sensed he was being watched, but then realised that his eye had been taken by a tall man who bounded from the stairwell, ran through the court and disappeared into the street. A tall man, in a black hat and cape.

'That was the Blackbird,' cried Titch.

'You sure?'

'Ay. Unmistakeable.'

'We must follow him.'

'Hey, Sam! The Creeper!' Sam whipped round to look, but the Creeper, too, had vanished. 'He's gone after the Blackbird, Sam.'

'I should follow them quick.'

'Shall I keep an eye on "the woman"?'

'If you're game, Titch. See you later. Take care.'

'And you, Sam. Be careful.'

Waving goodbye, Sam ran out into the street just in time to catch the Creeper turning the corner. On the trail now, Sam rubbed his hands.

'As Mr Holmes would say,' he muttered to himself, 'the game . . . is afoot!'

# 7

# LORD QUENTIN SCARSBURY

Alone in Fox Court, Titch felt nervous, and remained wedged into a corner to avoid being seen. It was some while before '*the* woman' appeared – if indeed the dashing male figure with the pencil moustache was her. Titch found it hard to believe that this sprightly, well-dressed man was in reality a woman – everything, except perhaps the height, was convincingly male. Was Sam right? Was this Irene Adler?

'The woman' walked fast, with long, masterful strides, swinging her cane, without a backward glance, allowing Titch to fall in a comfortable thirty to forty yards behind her. The mist gave cover. She obviously knew where she was going, pacing swiftly through Russell Square, past the University Quarter – Titch had to be careful not to lose her among the teeming students – and into Fitzrovia – the smarter residential area on the other side of Tottenham Court Road. Through the elegance of Fitzroy Square Titch kept close.

In Conway Street, 'the woman' slowed her pace, very soon spotting what she was looking for – a gentlemen's club – The Fitzroy. She stopped and looked round. Opposite The Fitzroy, on the other side of the street, was a mews, and into this unlit cul-de-sac 'the woman' disappeared.

Titch now had to be careful. As the mews was a dead-end, she daren't follow her quarry into it. Some light from the gas lamps in Conway Street spilled into the narrow mews entrance, making it hard for Titch even to look without giving herself away. She was keen to know what 'the woman' was doing in there, but it was risky.

Titch edged her way to the corner of the mews and peered cautiously into the darkness. What she saw made her heart leap in her chest. 'The woman' was there – *right* there – far too close for comfort. About three or four yards into the mews, she was standing with her shoulder to the wall. Her back was partly turned towards Titch – which was why she did not see her – and she was bending forward examining something.

Breathing a sigh of relief, Titch pulled back from the corner, retreating a few yards to safety. She needed to keep an eye on the entrance to the mews, in case 'the woman' emerged, so she crossed back over the street and hid in the entrance of a chandler's shop, a few doors along from The Fitzroy. From here Titch could see everything. She watched and waited, and wondered where Sam had got to.

Conway Street was quiet, too quiet. It was *so* quiet that Titch could hear a ticking from inside the chandler's shop, and the gentle chimes of a grandfather clock. Occasionally people came in and out of The Fitzroy. In an impressive purple coat, hat and gloves, the grand doorman emerged to summon cabs. Although the street attracted little traffic, the piercing blast of his whistle brought cabs within minutes, looming up suddenly through the swathes of thickening mist. On one occasion, two cabs arrived at the same time from different directions. As the first hansom took his passenger away, the second cab pulled up outside The Fitzroy and the doorman spoke to the driver.

'Stick around, you. I have an important guest leaving in a few minutes.' His manner was curt and superior. He went back into the club. The cab waited. Titch watched.

No one left the mews, which was perfectly placed, Titch calculated, for observing the discreet portico and revolving door of The Fitzroy, almost dead opposite. Titch concluded that 'the woman' was waiting for someone to leave, or perhaps arrive at, The Fitzroy. The mist, which had been growing denser since dusk, was turning to fog. Titch rubbed her hands against the cold, and continued to observe.

The doorman came out of The Fitzroy followed by a bulldog of a man who had an aura about him, a sense of self-importance. He sported a stylish top-hat, a floor-length overcoat with an astrakhan collar, and strode out of the revolving door, putting on his gloves like a performer taking the stage. Titch had a strange sense of foreboding that something unpleasant was about to occur. The doorman touched his cap and bowed slightly, fawning now.

'Cab ready and waiting, sir.'

'Thank you. Goodnight,' – the brusque superior tones of an aristocrat.

'Goodnight, Lord Scarsbury.'

Titch heard the name clearly. Scarsbury. Unmistakeable – Lord Scarsbury, the English nobleman suspected of stealing the Rose from the Astons in South Africa. Titch remembered, too that *with* Scarsbury on the night of the theft, had been none other than Irene Adler. 'If "the woman" hiding in the mews opposite is Irene Adler,' thought Titch, 'it's Lord Scarsbury she's waiting for.'

Frustratingly, the hansom-cab partly obscured Titch's view of the mews entrance. She was worried she might lose 'the woman' and decided she would have to move. As she was crossing the road Scarsbury barked, 'I shall be late.' His voice was both gruff and imperious.

'Don't worry, sir,' replied the doorman reassuringly.

'And much wealthier, I trust,' said Scarsbury, rubbing his now gloved fingers and thumb together – Titch assumed he was off to a casino. She stopped, sensing more sharply that something dangerous was about to happen. 'You shall have your commission later!' Scarsbury added in jest. The doorman laughed sycophantically, but the laughter died on his lips, for as he opened the hansom-cab door, a tall man emerged, holding a gun aimed directly at Scarsbury. Titch hovered in the middle of the street, frightened but fascinated, unable to tear herself away from the drama unfolding in front of the club. The tall man with the gun might have been the Blackbird, but Titch was too scared to go closer to find out. The doorman dived for cover – typical, thought Titch! Scarsbury, now a deathly white, was backing towards the revolving door of The Fitzroy. Titch heard the gunman say, 'You know what this is for.' As he spoke, he raised the gun, aiming it straight at Scarsbury's head.

There was a loud cry from further up the street, which momentarily distracted the would-be assassin. Then a shot rang out. Titch recoiled, expecting to see Scarsbury fall to the floor, but instead the gunman dropped his weapon, grabbed his arm and let loose a cry of anguish. Scarsbury, scrabbling back towards the club, was on the point of entering the revolving door, when the gunman, who had picked up the fallen gun with his good hand, succeeded in firing off another shot. The bullet narrowly missed Scarsbury and ricocheted off the spinning door.

At almost exactly the same moment, Titch heard a report from another gun. Where this third bullet was fired from was not clear, but Titch, who had made the cover of a doorway on the mews side of the street opposite The Fitzroy, saw the shell spray off the wall to the side of the revolving door, and heard it clatter away up the glistening cobblestones. Scarsbury by now had groped his way into the safety of the club.

The wounded gunman staggered back into his cab,

yelling angrily at the driver, and the horses galloped away, into the fogbound night. The doorman, recovering his lost topper from the gutter and smoothing down his purple coat, slid back into the club, glancing nervously after the retreating cab. Titch breathed a sigh of relief and turned her attention to 'the woman'.

Leaving her doorway, Titch edged along the street and looked round tentatively into the mews. Nothing. No one. She ventured timidly into the darkness, but there was no sign of anyone at all. She was about to emerge into Conway Street when she saw a figure approaching the club. Staying in the darkness of the mews, Titch watched as the man drew nearer. He looked about suspiciously, before entering the revolving door, and as he did so Titch recognised the Creeper. The Creeper – whom Sam had been following. Where then was Sam? In the excitement and fear, Titch had forgotten about him. And where was the Blackbird – whom the Creeper had been following? All vanished, like 'the woman', like Sam's coin.

Titch was cross with herself for losing her prey. 'The woman' wasn't in the mews and she hadn't passed Titch's doorway, so she must have gone the other way. Titch set off down Conway Street, her eyes on stalks.

She had not gone far when she paused to peer into another mews. It was even darker than the one she had just come from. Titch stared in but could see nothing, and was about to proceed when, from the darkness, she heard a muffled cry. Titch edged into the shadows, feeling her way, hands out in front of her like a blind person, afraid that she would bump into something in the blackness. The cries were stifled, indistinct, but getting louder. Titch wanted to turn and run, but felt drawn to discover the source of the desperate noises. Who could it be? 'The woman', maybe?

As her eyes adjusted to the opaque blackness of the mews, Titch became aware of someone on the pavement, gagged, and tied to the railings. Nervously Titch knelt down to the whining bundle. Feeling for the cords binding the struggling figure, she realised to her horror that it was Sam. His arms were tied behind his back, and the same rope secured his feet, tethering him to the railings in such a way that he was forced to squat.

'Sam! Are you all right?' said Titch, struggling to undo the tightly bound gag. Sam nodded, as Titch fought to loosen the vicious knots at his neck. She couldn't shift them. Working in the dark didn't help. Nodding and grunting, Sam indicated that Titch

123

should try the binding on the railings, and after something of a fight, this eventually gave way. Sam was then able to stand up. Hopping, to get his legs working again, he shook off the ropes from his hands and ankles, and began wrestling with the gag. Titch felt helpless, but Sam managed finally to wrench it off and remove the ball of cloth that had been shoved into his mouth. He spat it out, free at last to breathe easily.

'Sam, are you all right?'

'Thank goodness you found me, Titch,' he retched. 'I heard gunshots. What the hell's been going on?'

They huddled together in the darkness. Titch rubbed Sam's wrists as she filled him in on the shooting.

'I need to get a look at where it happened, Titch. Quick.' Before she could move, Sam took Titch's face in his hands. He looked at her with relief and gratitude. 'Thanks for finding me. Come on. Quick.' He ran out of the mews, hobbling a little.

'Hang on, Sam. You're going too fast for yourself.'

'There's no time, Titch, I've got to take a look before the police get here.'

'What for?' asked Titch, running after him.

But Sam was in no mood to answer. He reached The Fitzroy and started examining the ground in the vicinity of the revolving door. When Titch caught up with him, he demanded, 'Where were the shots fired from, Titch?'

'It all happened so fast, I'm not sure where they came *from*, but one bullet hit the door.'

They immediately spotted the splintered gash on the wooden base of the revolving door where the bullet had struck. They stood for a moment working out its trajectory. Without warning, Sam fell to his knees and was off, crawling about frantically, searching the pavement. Titch hovered patiently, uncomfortably. She could see people gathering around Lord Scarsbury in the foyer of the club. Fortunately, they were apprehensive about coming outside, and were being discouraged from doing so by the doorman. This gave Sam a few moments in which to search unhindered.

Suddenly he cried, 'Got it!' He stood up, holding out his hand to Titch. In it was a bullet casing. 'That's *one*,' he cried elatedly. 'I heard three shots: you said one hit the gunman, I've got *this* one. There must be one more.'

'It hit the wall. I heard it spin up this way.' Titch led Sam up the street.

Again Sam was down on his knees, crawling about like a madman, his eyes close to the ground. Titch became aware of the sound of running feet, and two policemen emerged through the fog, rounding the corner fifty yards away, beyond The Fitzroy.

'Quick, Sam. The police are here.' Another policeman appeared from the other direction. Undeterred, unaware, Sam continued to scour the pavement.

'Got it!' he cried triumphantly, leaping to his feet. 'Let's go.'

They shot across the street and disappeared into the mews opposite The Fitzroy. Sheltered here, they watched the police go in. The moment their way was free, Sam and Titch were out of the mews and running. It took them no more than fifteen minutes to reach Baker Street, but as they were approaching 221b, Sam said, 'Titch, I think we should keep this to ourselves. We can't tell the Doc – he'd kill us. And if we tell Billy, it'll put him in a tricky position. Let's get back to our place.'

'Ay. You're right.'

So they set off for their secret room. Titch was concerned that Sam had shrugged the whole event off so quickly. He was sore from the ropes and the gag, but otherwise he seemed unaffected. Back in their hide-away, Titch was at last able to ask him how he had come to be trussed up, and who had done it.

'Well,' said Sam, 'I set off following the Creeper – and it was easy, you know – it's turning foggy, and he's concentrating on trailing the Blackbird. We get to Fitzroy Square, and he stops. He just stands there. It felt like he'd lost his man – or arrived at where he was going, know what I mean? It's a while before he starts off again, and when I get round the corner into Conway Street – where the club is – there's no sign of either of them. I just walk down past the club hoping to catch sight of the Creeper, when this hand comes out the dark and grabs me.'

'Did you see who it was, Sam?'

'Are you kidding?'

'The Creeper?'

'And how! He gags me and ties me up like you found me – he was dead quick and strong – boy, he was strong – and when he's finished, he gets out a gun. I thought he was going to kill me. He sticks it under my nose, and says, "Keep out of this, kid. You *and* your little friends. Next time . . ." and he rams the gun into my cheek – is there a mark?'

Titch held the candle close to Sam's face. 'Ay, there is. A scratch and a bit of a bruise. Does it hurt?'

'Not much. Anyway, "Next time," he says, "there won't *be* a next time. Comprendi?" It was terrifying,

'Titch. I never been so scared.'

'It *is* terrifying, Sam. One of us is going to get hurt. I keep thinking of the dead body in Edie's vision.'

'I know. But the point is, Titch, I reckon it was the Creeper that fired the first shot. Listen. He finished with me and disappeared for ages. When he came back, he was all tense. He had his gun in his hand and he suddenly took off up the street, yelling. This was just before the first shot. I think it was *his* shot that hit the gunman in the arm. Right?'

'Ay. He would have been able to see the gunman clearly, coming up that way.'

'And did it save Scarsbury?'

'Ay. If it hadn't been for that shot, Scarsbury would have got it smack in the head.'

'So . . . maybe the Creeper's job is to *protect* Scarsbury from someone.' Sam thought about this for a moment.

'Hey, Sam, I've just remembered. Before he was hit, the gunman said to Scarsbury, "*You know what this is for.*"'

'That's interesting.' Sam repeated the words. '*You know what this is for.* Who do you think the gunman was, Titch?'

'Not sure. Might have been the Blackbird.'

'It wouldn't half help if we knew.'

'I didn't get too close because of the guns.'

'Course.'

'So I can't be certain if it was the Blackbird or not. What *happened* to him Sam?'

'Disappeared. Never saw him after Fitzroy Square. And the woman?'

'Vanished.'

'This case drives me nuts, Titch. If it weren't for Potts, I'd give up.'

'Perhaps we *should* give up.'

'And let Hector hang? We can't, Titch, can we?'

'No. We can't.' Titch was still curious. 'Sam. The Creeper fired the first shot, and the gunman fired the second. Who fired the third?'

'Well, that's why I wanted to get the bullet casings. I must get them to Lestrade . . .'

'He won't help, Sam!'

'He'll *have* to. By now, the police should have done the autopsy.'

'The what?'

'You know, the examination on the body of the Shift Manager. And I've got a theory, Titch.'

'What?'

He fished the casings out of his pocket. 'If one of

these bullets matches the one they take out of the Shift Manager, that means it was fired from the same gun. Right?'

'Right.'

'And the gun that killed the Shift Manager has the initials I.A. on it. Right?'

'Right.'

'And who was hiding in the mews opposite The Fitzroy? In a perfect position to shoot at someone going in or out?'

'The woman.'

'Her-very-blooming-self. Miss Irene Adler. I'm right, aren't I?'

'You could be,' said Titch.

'It was *her* gun that fired the bullet that killed the Shift Manager, Titch. I'm certain. She was there, in the vaults with Hector. And if we can stick cold proof under Lestrade's nose, he *must* help. He can't let an innocent man go to his death *knowing* he's innocent, can he?'

'I wish I had your faith, Sam,' said Titch despondently.

'We've got to try and see Lestrade in the morning.'

'Without Dr Watson's help?'

''Fraid so.'

'That won't be easy. Not after your last run-in with him.'

'I'm hoping Potts's dad can help us there. Let's try and get some shut-eye – it's going to be a busy morning. First . . . we have a word with Potts and Edie at Marylebone, then we get Potts's dad on board, then we go see Lestrade. And then . . . blow the candle out, Titch . . .' he said, snuggling under his blanket and drawing it up to his chin, '. . . and then . . . I want to see Old Charvis again.'

They settled down in the dark, but neither of them felt like sleep. After a few minutes that seemed like hours, Sam said, 'Titch.'

'Ay?'

'What did the gunman look like?'

'Didn't see his face. He were quite tall, though.'

'Was he?'

'Ay.'

'He wasn't wearing a black cape, was he?'

'I told you, I couldn't see properly. The cab was in the way.'

'When I trailed the Creeper and the Blackbird, the Blackbird just disappeared. Never saw him after Fitzroy Square.'

'I wonder where he got to.'

'Exactly.'

There was a long silence.

'Titch.'

'Ay?'

'Who do we know who's tall?'

'The Blackbird?'

'And who was the Creeper following?'

'The Blackbird.'

'So who do you reckon tried to shoot Scarsbury?'

'The man in the moon.'

'Don't be daft.'

They were quiet again for some time.

'Sam.'

'Yeah?'

'Nothing is what it seems. Remember?'

'Dead right, Titch. Not one single bloomin' thing.'

# 8

# NOTHING IS WHAT IS SEEMS

Potts and Edie were unsure what to do. Sam and Titch had come by early and asked them to keep an eye on Old Charvis. Potts wasn't running for Jacky Dyke, and Edie was confident they would sell out early – the surprise of a bright, sunny winter morning after the previous night's fog had put people in a good mood and trade was brisk. Potts was desperate to help Hector, and in principle they were free to watch Charvis, but since Watson's stern warning, the growing dangers of the case, and Edie's disturbing vision of an upside-down dead body, they were nervous of doing more until Sherlock Holmes returned.

When Sam and Titch left Marylebone Station, they weren't convinced that Potts and Edie were going to help.

'Not to worry, Titch,' said Sam. 'We'll get over to Charvis's place ourselves as soon as this thing with Lestrade is over. Let's go find Potts's dad.'

Potts had told them when his dad would be coming to the end of his beat in Trafalgar Square. It didn't take long to spot him with his fellow constable – shooing a couple of kids off the lions. Mr Potts said that as soon as he was free he would go with them to see Lestrade – anything to help Hector.

Scotland Yard, the new headquarters of the Metropolitan Police, was an intimidating Gothic structure – a huge building on Victoria Embankment. Even Potts's dad was unnerved by it.

'D'you know,' he said as they approached, 'they found a woman's torso in the cellar one night when they were building this place? It gives me the creeps.'

In they all went, and Mr Potts used his position to get a message to Inspector Lestrade, who appeared eventually, looking annoyed. He was particularly miffed to see Sam again.

'What can I do for you?' Lestrade asked.

Mr Potts said they had some evidence from the shooting outside The Fitzroy which might be useful in Hector's defence. Inspector Lestrade had in fact just returned from the crime scene. Sam kept very quiet, but because Titch was able to provide eye-witness *details* of the incident, Lestrade grudgingly took them upstairs to his rather grand office overlooking the river to take notes. The autopsy, he informed them, had been performed on the Shift Manager, and he showed them the bullet taken from his body. Next to it, Sam laid the two casings he had found in the street outside the club. As he had predicted, one of them was a perfect match for the bullet that had killed Hector's boss.

In spite of himself, Lestrade could not help but be impressed. He looked at Sam in a somewhat different light, listening attentively this time as he developed his theory that it was Miss Irene Adler's pearl-handled pistol that had fired the matching bullets.

'It's all connected with the Rose, Inspector,' said Sam. 'Lord Scarsbury stole it from the Astons in South Africa, and got away with it. *He* deposited it in the vaults at the African Diamond Company – Billy checked and his name's on the register. Irene Adler was *with* him at the time of the theft, and —'

'I don't quite see the relevance —'

'The real point is, sir, if Hector was really guilty, why would anyone try and bump him off? No. The guilty person is afraid he'll spill the beans. Irene Adler's gun killed the Shift Manager. I believe she tried to get rid of Hector to protect herself. The gun's been stolen from here, and she used it again last night outside The Fitzroy. Titch saw her. There's the proof.' Sam indicated the bullet casings. 'I also think she's got the Rose. We're desperate to save Hector, sir – this gentleman's brother – and you're the only one who can help.'

'Well,' puffed Lestrade, 'I dislike you interfering in police matters, Master Wiggins, but in this instance you do appear to know what you're talking about.'

Mr Potts raised his hand politely. 'Do you mind if I say something, Inspector?' Lestrade shook his head. 'My brother, 'Ector,' said Mr Potts deliberately, 'did not commit this murder. I *know* we can't prove it – but you can take my word for it – 'e didn't do it. 'E's takin' the rap for someone else. These 'ere lads have been trying to 'elp, cos they know 'ow as it's unjust. And they've done bloomin' well, if you ask me. All we ask is that you make sure that 'Ector don't get shoved off to the gallows before we have time to prove 'e's given a false confession. That's why we took the liberty of coming 'ere, and we're very grateful to you for 'earin' us out. Come on, lads. The Inspector's got the bullets. 'E's a busy man, and we should let 'im get on. Thank you, sir. Good morning.' This very proper speech was quite the longest Mr Potts had ever delivered, and when it was over, he led the two boys away.

It was midday. Outside, the bracing winter sun had been replaced by thick cloud. Mr Potts walked back to Soho with Sam and Titch, then set off home, whilst they headed, as planned, for Old Charvis's attic in Cripplegate Square.

Mounting the ladder to Old Charvis's door, Titch whispered, 'I think there's something wrong, Sam. What's that smell?'

'Iodine, isn't it?'

'Ay.'

'You're right, Titch. Something's happened.'

Sam knocked on the door, which was opened, to his amazement, by Potts.

'Fank God you're 'ere! Come in.' Potts hauled Titch and Sam into the room, where they saw to their dismay that something had indeed happened: Old Charvis was stretched out on the bed with a blanket over him; Edie was sitting, holding his hand. There was a bandage round the old boy's head with a bloodstain on it. The room smelled strongly of iodine. Recalling Edie's vision, they feared he might be dead, but to their relief he stirred. Sam bounded over to look at him.

'Hi, Edie. What's been going on?'

'Sure, Potts'll tell you. I'm keeping an eye on the old boy.'

'Well,' said Potts, 'when we got 'ere, 'e didn't answer the door, and we nearly went away, but then we 'eard 'im groaning'. 'E was on the floor, bruised and bleedin' – and the place was a mess – it still is but we done our best. 'E couldn't walk, but we managed to drag 'im on to the bed. I grabbed some dough from 'is pocket and went out for bandages and iodine and a drop of laudanum. Edie cleaned 'im up, and 'e's a lot better.'

'Had the carpet been moved?' enquired Sam.

Potts was surprised by the question. 'No. Why?'

'Tell you later. Can he talk?'

''E can a bit now. I mean this was a coupla 'ours ago. I nearly went for the Doc but 'e wouldn't want us to be 'ere at all so I didn't like to, know what I mean?'

'Listen. You've both done brilliant. And thanks for coming. We weren't sure you would. Could I have a word with the old boy?'

'Wot d'you reckon, Edie?'

'Sure, come on over. Give it a go.'

Sam edged to the top of the bed and leaned

down over the feeble figure.

'Mr Charvis.' The old man twitched. Sam tried once more, louder. 'Mr Charvis. Look at me.' After a moment, Sam found himself peering into a pair of very old, very confused eyes.

'Who are you?' Charvis breathed.

'It's me. Sam.'

'Who?'

'The boy who knows about diamonds. Sam!'

'Ah! Sam. I had forgotten . . . Sam, dear boy . . .' His eyes closed slowly, his head lolled to one side, and he was quiet.

'Mr Charvis. Who did this to you?' Charvis didn't respond. 'Who did this?' Sam repeated, but Charvis had drifted away from him, back into semi-consciousness. 'Poor old thing. *I'll* keep an eye on him for a bit now, and have a think. Titch, fill Edie and Potts in on everything.'

Sam sat watching and thinking. Old Charvis slept as Titch recounted the previous night's shooting and their visit to Scotland Yard. They admitted they were all increasingly afraid, but in the end, they agreed they must continue to help Hector. They felt bad that Billy was being left out because they were avoiding Dr Watson. Edie said she would see him on the way home and bring him up to date. She and Potts were, frankly, relieved to go.

Whether it was pain or his dreams of a new life that caused Old Charvis to moan occasionally, it was impossible to say, but when he woke, he tried to sit up. Sam and Titch went to him

'Who are *you*?' he asked.

'It's me, sir. Sam.'

'Who?'

'The boy who knows about diamonds.'

'Oh, Sam. I keep forgettin'. Dear Sam. And this is . . . Edie?' he said, peering at Titch.

'No, sir, this is my friend Titch.'

'Oh, Titch. How grand. What *would* I do without you all?' Old Charvis took Sam urgently by the arm and pulled him close. 'Dear boy, would you be so kind as to perform a small favour for me? *Another* favour, I should say.' He was breathing unevenly. His lips were cracked, white at the edges, and his voice reedy and feeble. Titch offered him the drink that Edie had left. He sipped at it greedily, and went on. 'Could you deliver a message for me?'

'Of course, sir. What?'

'Might you nip round to Fox Court – do you know where—'

'I do, sir. Off the Gray's Inn Road.'

'Good boy. There is a lady to whom I need to convey a message of the utmost importance. Main stairway, second floor, middle back.' Sam waited with bated breath. That was exactly where he had encountered 'the woman' – Irene Adler. He sensed that Charvis was going to ask him to visit her. He found it hard to swallow and his heart began thumping in his chest. 'Kindly locate this lady, dear Sam, and tell her from me, *It is ready*. Do you follow?'

'Yes, sir. That's easy.'

'*It is ready*. And, *She can collect it. As soon as she likes.*' His grip on Sam's arm loosened, and his long thin face crinkled into a wide smile of deep contentment.

'Just one thing, sir,' said Sam – his mouth dry with apprehension – 'the lady's name?'

'Ah, yes, of course. Don't want you givin' it to the wrong person, do we?'

'No, sir.'

'The lady's name . . .' He pulled Sam close again and whispered hoarsely, 'is . . . Constance Lord.'

Sam's jaw dropped. In the breathing of that name, all his theories collapsed. Charvis asked Sam to repeat the name. Through lips that barely moved Sam mouthed the words, 'Constance Lord.'

'*Lady* Constance Lord, I should say,' said Charvis as he lay back, exhausted by the effort, and again fell fast asleep.

Sam put his head in his hands. 'I'm wrong, Titch. I've got it all wrong. It's her – Fox Court, second floor, middle back. It's her, but her name is *not* Irene Adler. Who *is* she? I mean, what's going on?'

'I don't get it, Sam.'

'What about the photo, though? It's her!'

'On this case, Sam, remember . . . nothing is what it seems.'

'Dead right.'

'Perhaps she's just using a false name,' said Titch. 'Why don't you get this message out the way, and then we can work out what to do next?'

Sam was baffled and downcast. Titch was upset for him. She put her hand on his shoulder and said, 'Shall I stay here – keep an eye on himself?' They turned to gaze at the long thin figure on the bed. The old man's mouth was open, his chin sagging, his upper teeth protruding strangely. If it hadn't been for the feeble rise and fall of his chest, you might have thought the old boy had passed away. He looked dead.

'Poor old thing.'

'Poor old thing. See you later, Titch. Keep an ear open

in case whoever did him over decides to come back.'

And with that, he left. Titch watched him descend the creaky ladder, and then carefully locked the door.

As Sam neared Fox Court, he felt numb with disbelief. He was absolutely certain that the woman he had met, the woman they had followed disguised as a man, was Irene Adler. Where had he gone wrong? Standing outside the fated door where he had encountered her, he was surprised to hear noises from within – sounds of children and shouting. He rapped hard. The door was opened by a large woman, grubbily dressed in ragged clothes. A dirty child – naked save for a wrap round his waist – clung to her. Sam was stunned.

The woman was unsympathetic. 'Yes?'

Sam asked if a Miss Lord lived there.

'Lord?' said the woman. 'Lord! 'Ere? You won't find any nobs in this dump!' She laughed raucously.

'I spoke to her,' Sam persevered. 'She was here only yesterday.'

'Well, she left only this morning, didn't she?'

'Do you know where she went?'

'I'll get the boss. 'E carried 'er bags for 'er. She paid 'im 'n' all.' As the woman shuffled off, the child stuck his tongue out at Sam. Their place was taken by a man wearing filthy trousers and a torn, stained vest, who looked suspiciously at Sam. 'What d'you wanna know, kid?'

'I've got a message for Lady, er, *Miss* Constance Lord.'

Sensing there might be more money in it, the man asked, 'D' you wanna leave it wi' me?'

'No, thank you, sir. I need to tell her in person.'

'Oh, all right then.' Unwillingly, he told Sam where Miss Lord had moved to – an address in Holborn. Sam thanked him and set off wearily. The wind was sharp and he felt he was wasting time when he really needed to get back to Titch and rethink.

He found Cloak Lane easily, in a nicer, much smarter area, but as he turned into the street, he was shaken by the sight of a man partially concealed behind a newspaper, standing almost opposite number 19, the grand house that was Sam's destination. Immediately suspicious, Sam took cover in the porch of an office building on the corner. From here, through the fading afternoon light, he could observe the man, who seemed rooted to the spot. When the man lowered his newspaper, and moved, Sam recognised him immediately. A shiver of fear ran through him, for if there was one person in the world he did not wish to encounter, it was this man, the man who had thrust a gun in his face only last night – the man they referred to as the Creeper.

Sam dared not approach the house while the Creeper was there, which at least gave him time to try and sort things out. Initially, he concluded he was not alone in having traced Lady Constance Lord to her new accommodation, but then the thought came to him that last night, protecting Scarsbury, the Creeper had not trailed the woman – but the Blackbird. Perhaps the Creeper was *still* trailing the Blackbird. Perhaps the Creeper was here because the Blackbird also lived at 19 Cloak Lane. Who *was* the Blackbird, the man in the black cape? And what was the relationship between the woman and the Blackbird? Questions, questions. Every minute Sam felt more and more out of his depth.

The Creeper changed position twice, eventually moving out of sight round the curve of the road. Sam seized his chance. He ran to the door and sounded the bell. While waiting, he noticed a brass plate on the wall – Broadwaters House. From within he could hear a piano and the dulcet lilt of a woman's voice, raised in song. It was the most exquisite voice – pure but strong. Unhurried, she finished her phrase. Had it not been for the beauty of the song, Sam might have run away. He

146

looked feverishly up and down the street, afraid that the Creeper would reappear and spot him. He was about to go when the front door opened. He turned. It was her – in an elegant dress, with a cashmere shawl over her shoulders the woman from Fox Court, the woman he thought of as Irene Adler. Confronted again by her clear blue eyes, Sam was hypnotised.

'Miss Lord?' he said mystified. '*Lady* Lord, I should say. Sorry – Lady Lord sounds odd,' he mumbled. 'Lady Constance, I mean.' He stopped, feeling foolish.

She smiled amiably at him. 'So today, sweet boy, you know my name.' Her warm beguiling voice further entranced him.

'Yes, your ladyship,' Sam stammered.

'Miss Lord will do.'

'Yes, Miss Lord.' He stood there, captivated by her pallid beauty, unable to speak.

'Well, sweet boy, I am waiting.'

'Sorry. I've got a message. It's from a Mr Charvis.'

She raised a finger to her lips. 'Sssh.' Her eyes flicked hurriedly up and down the street. 'Come in,' she said. Sam did not move. 'Quick, sweet boy. Come in.'

In a trance Sam drifted into the house.

# 9

# LADY CONSTANCE LORD

S am was led into the empty front room. Inside, Broadwaters House was elegant, but its charms had faded. He gazed in wonder at the ancient piano. He was confused. Lady Constance looked exactly like the woman he had met at Fox Court. The light blue of her eyes was unmistakable. Whether or not she was the woman involved in the shooting he had no way of knowing. His thoughts were interrupted by her gentle, honeyed voice.

'So, sweet boy, what is your message from this Mr Charvis?'

She looked at him so tenderly, Sam found it difficult to speak. 'He says, *It's ready.*'

'Is that all, sweet boy?'

'Yes, miss. No. Sorry. *It's ready . . .* and, *You can*

*collect it. As soon as you like.'*

'Thank you, sweet boy.' She turned towards the door. Sam thought she was about to show him out, but after standing for a moment, thinking, she said, 'Might I offer you a small reward for your good service?'

'I don't want money, thank you, miss.'

'I didn't mean money, sweet boy. Would you not like a nice warm seat by the kitchen range, and a mug of hot tea? It is windy out, and turning cold.'

'That would be most acceptable, miss. It's real parky today.'

She smiled and ushered him into the hall. He looked round for any evidence that would help him fix her identity. The house felt unlived in. There were no small every day items lying about. There was a large landscape painting entitled 'Tanga-Tanga' – treeless wastes of dry grass, a squat farmstead, and a river. There were a few garments on the cloak stand: among them, Sam noted, a black cape.

'Come along,' said Lady Constance, starting downstairs. The thick wallpaper in the stairwell was peeling and there were damp patches around the door leading to the garden. Lady Constance looked back up at Sam and smiled. As he edged down the scrubbed, wooden stairs to the basement, Sam felt he was being lured into an underground den. 'Where did you get that nasty bruise on your cheek?' she asked. 'You didn't have that yesterday.' Sam mumbled something about a fall. 'Did you find the woman you were looking for? I don't recall her name.'

'Miss Adler,' said Sam sullenly. 'No. I didn't.'

Again, she smiled. 'What is *your* name, sweet boy?'

'Sam Wiggins, miss.'

She started, then smoothed the front of her skirt, and placed a chair close to the range. 'Sit there in the warm while I make your tea.' Sam did as he was told. She lit the oil lamp and pushed the kettle on to the heat. With her back to Sam, she asked casually, 'Why were you looking for this Miss Adler?'

Sam took a deep breath. He needed to be careful. 'Well . . . It's a long story. A friend of mine's uncle has been charged with murder,' he began warily. 'He didn't do it, although he swears he did – nothing can shift him. I was trying to find Miss Adler to see if she might testify on his behalf.'

Busying herself with Sam's tea, still turned away from him, Lady Constance asked, 'Do you infer, sweet Sam,' she spoke his name tenderly, 'that if your friend's uncle maintains his . . . his lie, it will cost him his life?'

'Yes, miss.'

'Why then does he not change his testimony?'

'He's protecting Miss Adler is my theory, the woman I was trying to find. He's an honourable man. Very religious.'

With her hand on the large kettle, which was now boiling vigorously, Lady Constance asked, 'Will nothing persuade him to change his mind?'

'No, miss. He's very stubborn.'

She digested this remark slowly before speaking. 'What made you think I was Miss Adler?'

'Well, miss, I've seen this photograph of her. And she's very like you. Very . . .' Sam nearly said 'beautiful' but stopped himself. Embarrassed, he began to mumble again, 'It's a face you just don't forget, like. I thought it was you.'

In silence, Lady Constance made the tea.

'How old are you, Sam Wiggins?'

'Thirteen, miss.'

Sam heard an intake of breath. Then she asked, 'Would you like sugar, sweet Sam?'

'I don't often have the choice, but if you've got some . . . yes, thanks.'

She put two spoonfuls of sugar in the tea, stirred it and handed it to Sam. Sam looked up at her. 'Thank you, miss. Very kind.' He couldn't take his eyes off her, but he didn't take the mug.

'Take it,' she snapped. Sam couldn't. 'Take it.'

'You're crying, miss.'

She thrust the mug towards him. He grabbed it, splashing the tea, burning his thigh. She turned her back on him, took a handkerchief from her sleeve, and dabbed her eyes with it.

The tea was too hot to drink. Sam sat warming his hands on the mug. 'I'm sorry, miss. I didn't mean to upset you.'

Without responding, she walked slowly to the far end of the kitchen, so that Sam could not see her face. 'I had a son,' she said. 'He died when he was a baby. He would have been your age. His name was Sam.'

'I'm sorry.'

'Drink your tea.'

Sam tried to drink, but the tea was still too hot. As he sat, blowing on it, he heard again, in his mind, the woman's exquisite singing, and in an instant he knew. 'You *are* her, aren't you, miss?' he said quietly. She did not react. 'You are . . . Irene Adler.' They were both still. Eventually she turned and broke the long silence.

'What on earth makes you think that?'

With dry mouth and faltering tongue, Sam persevered. 'The photograph, mainly. Plus, I read about you . . . you're a singer, aren't you? You were. I heard you singing just now. The most beautiful thing I ever heard.' Still the woman did not respond. 'If I'm wrong,' said Sam cautiously, 'I'm real sorry, but if . . . if it *is* you . . . if you *are* Irene Adler . . . it's you my friend's uncle is trying to protect, and—'

'Drink your tea,' she said. Her tone was harder – she wasn't calling him 'sweet boy' or 'sweet Sam' now.

Sam suspected he had gone too far. 'Perhaps you could put a spot more milk in it, please, miss, it's dead hot.'

'Help yourself. The jug with the lace doily.'

Sam got up and, trembling slightly, took another cooling drop of milk. The silence was broken only by the beads on the doily chinking against the china jug. He began to drink.

'Don't make such a noise.'

'Sorry, miss. I'm rushing.' He tried not to slurp his tea, but it was hard to concentrate, even on so simple a thing as drinking, with *her* there. *Was* this Irene Adler? She had not denied it. Sherlock Holmes's words were ringing in Sam's ears – Irene Adler was the only woman he had ever met capable of murder. Was he alone with a murderess? Under her spell, Sam found it hard to believe that this woman was a killer. She made him uneasy, but he felt drawn to her. 'You know your house is being watched, miss?'

'Oh?'

'There was a man opposite with a newspaper. A short, sturdy man. Great black boots and a big moustache.'

'You don't miss much, do you, Sam Wiggins?'

Sam drained the mug. 'I don't wish to interfere, miss . . . thank you for my nice tea. I like sugar.' He placed the empty mug on the table.

'The man you noticed Sam is a private detective who has been hired by . . . by someone who wishes us ill.' Sam noticed that she said 'us'. Once more she dabbed her eyes with her handkerchief. 'His name is Uriah Pogue. Do not go anywhere near him.'

Sam was tempted to say he had already been far *too* near him.

She looked sadly at him. 'Sweet Sam, I would like you to do something for me. Would you?' Sam knew that she was being nice to him again because she wanted something. Perhaps this was her real reason for offering him tea. She replaced the handkerchief in her sleeve. 'I think I can trust you, can't I?'

'It depends, miss.' Sam was fighting his instinct to give in to her. 'The thing is, if you want me to do something for you, I think you should be straight with me, please, miss.'

Her clear blue eyes narrowed slightly. 'For a sweet boy, you drive a hard bargain.'

'It's very important to me to help my friend, miss.'

'Of course. If you do this small thing for me, I promise I will make everything clear. Will you help a lady in distress?'

Sam hovered, uncertain. She moved to the oil lamp and dowsed the flame. There was barely any light now in the room. She came towards him, her light blue eyes piercing in the gloom. Her nearness unnerved him.

'What exactly do you want me to do, miss?' he asked hesitantly.

'Thank you, sweet Sam. I knew you would come to my rescue.' She was so close to him now he could smell her delicate violet scent. 'I would like you to tell dear old Mr Charvis that he may . . . *give it to you*. I would like you to bring it to me. Do you understand?' Sam nodded. 'That won't be too difficult, will it, Sam?' Sam shook his head. 'There.' She placed her hand on his cheek. 'Can you climb a wall, Sam?'

The question surprised him. 'I have been known to, miss. Why?'

'Because you should leave here without being seen by nasty Mr Pogue – it would be safer for you.' She stroked his bruise with her thumb. 'Sweet Sam.' Her eyes were locked on Sam's, but he sensed that she saw, not him, but the ghost of her dead son. He shivered. She brushed past him. At the turn in the stair, she looked back and smiled. 'Wait for me in the hall.'

As he followed her up the stairs out of the darkened kitchen, Sam felt as though he was escaping from a snare. He stood in the hall, waiting, observing. He caught sight of himself in a huge gold-framed mirror looking out of place and vulnerable. The black cape, he noticed, was no longer on the cloak stand.

After a few minutes, the woman emerged from the piano-room holding an envelope. Blowing gently to dry the ink, she again came very close to Sam. 'Let me give you this, sweet Sam,' she said intimately, opening his jacket and sliding the envelope into his inside pocket. 'There. Make *very* sure not to lose it.' She was telling him, quite plainly, that it contained money. 'Give it to Mr Charvis, and he will let you have a small package for me. I shall wait here . . . just for you . . . sweet Sam.' Sam nodded. 'I observed just now that pesky Mr Pogue has returned to his post, so if you are game for a little mountaineering, perhaps you will follow me.'

She led him into the garden. Flakes of snow had begun to settle. She offered to help him on to the wall, but Sam leaped up before she could touch him. 'How clever,' she remarked, looking up at him astride the wall.

Sam's eye was drawn to a light at the top of the house. Silhouetted in an upstairs window was a man watching them, a man wearing a cape.

'The owner of the house,' came her casual explanation.

Sam looked down. 'Shall I come back this way when I bring the package, miss?'

'You *are* clever. Do.' Sam was about to jump off the wall when she reached up to him. 'You are the only person who can help me, sweet Sam. Don't fail me.'

Sam took one last look into the haunting blue of her eyes, and, without answering, slid over the wall.

# 10

# EDIE'S VISION

Old Charvis barely moved. Watching his shallow breathing, and waiting patiently for Sam, Titch became aware of sounds outside the room, and tiptoed to the door.

'Who is it?' Titch demanded. There was no reply, but Titch knew there was someone out there. 'Who *is* it?' Titch asked again, louder.

'It's Billy!' came the reply. 'Open up!'

Titch unlocked the door. 'Billy! What you doing here? Come in.' Billy scrambled into the room. 'You didn't half give me a scare.'

'Sorry. Edie told me what was going on, and I thought you might need a bit of support.'

'Thanks. What about your mum?'

'I told her I was working late at Baker Street.' Billy

noticed Old Charvis. 'How is he?'

'Asleep,' said Titch. 'He's a sweet old feller. I've got quite fond of him.'

Old Charvis called out in his sleep, a feeble cry. They moved to either side of his bed. His eyes were still closed.

'What shall we do, Titch? Spend the night here? See he's all right?'

'I guess. And wait for Sam.'

'I thought he'd be here with you.'

'He's gone to deliver something for the old boy.'

Old Charvis stirred as if he knew they were watching him. Suddenly, he sat up, his eyes staring. He did not speak. Titch and Billy laid him gently back down again.

'Who are you?' he asked, eyes still staring.

'Friends of Sam, sir.'

'Who?'

'Sam – the boy you sent on an errand.'

'Oh, Sam. Is he back yet?'

'No, sir. We're waiting for him.'

'Is he safe, d'you think?' Old Charvis seemed troubled by his sudden fear for Sam.

'I'm sure he is, sir.'

'I'm worried about him,' he said, panic rising.

Billy and Titch were trying to comfort the old boy when they became aware that someone was trying to open the door. Old Charvis heard it too. All three of them froze.

'Is it locked, Titch?' Billy whispered.

'Not 'alf.'

'Who can it be?'

'Maybe it's Sam,' said Old Charvis hopefully.

As weight was evidently being applied to the door to force it open, Billy and Titch were inclined to think otherwise. Then there was a violent hammering, followed by an angry voice: 'Let me in, Charvis.'

The old man suddenly realised there was danger. 'It sounds as though the unpleasant man who did this to me,' said Old Charvis, placing a hand on his bandaged head, 'has returned. You two had better hide.' He indicated a torn curtain, under the eaves at the top of his bed. 'Behind that,' he said, 'there's a cupboard. Go on. Quick.'

Whoever was outside was growing impatient. There was a repeated banging. The key fell out of the door and clattered to the floor – and then, as Titch and Billy slipped behind the curtain, one of the door panels began to split.

\* \* \*

As he made his way back to Old Charvis's Sam was wary – checking constantly to make sure that the Creeper – Uriah Pogue – at least he now knew his name – was not on his tail. The heavy cloud had turned to snow, which slowed him down. As he tramped, he tried to organise his thoughts. He was convinced that Lady Constance was Irene Adler: in Watson's story, Irene Adler was a singer – Sam could not get her singing out of his mind. *And* there was the photograph. Lady Constance was roughly the same build as the man Titch had followed last night. She had been living in Fox Court, and she had moved the moment Sam was on to her, which suggested she had something to hide. It *had* to be Irene Adler.

Trudging down Gray's Inn Road, hardly aware of the falling snow, Sam was gripped by the notion that nothing, as Titch kept reminding him, was what it seemed: fake jewellery, false names, good people like Hector telling lies, nice people who couldn't be trusted. Schneid was the word Ruben Curtis had used. Schneid – counterfeit. Fake. Sam remembered the phantom-like image of the caped figure in the upstairs window. The Blackbird. Did he own Broadwaters House, as 'the woman' claimed? Was this a clue or another lie? Sam forced his muddled thoughts back to the question of

Irene Adler. What did he actually know about her?

Irene Adler had been with Scarsbury on the night the Rose was stolen from the Astons in South Africa. Irene Adler had been with Hector when it 'disappeared' from the vaults of the African Diamond Company. 'Constance Lord *is* Irene Adler, and I think *she's* got the Rose now,' Sam said to himself. 'But if she's got it, why does she need Old Charvis? Questions. Questions. And no bloomin' answers.' Sam kicked at the deepening snow in frustration, and pushed on.

Behind the curtain, Titch and Billy discovered a hinged panel which opened into a long, shallow cupboard under the eaves. Billy was nudging it open when they heard the room door splintering. The cupboard was so narrow and low Billy had to squeeze in one way and Titch the other. Being on the pudgy side it was quite tight for Billy, squirming hurriedly into the dust, and mess of small boxes and papers. Titch slid in more easily, feet first, in order to shut the panel behind them. As Titch closed it, there was a loud crash, and the door to the room gave way completely. They heard footsteps as the intruder came in.

Cramped in the dark, neither Titch nor Billy could work out what was happening. Although they could hear a man's voice – not shouting, but threatening, menacing – they couldn't make out the words. They could hear Charvis pleading. There were the sounds of a struggle, of the bed itself moving – scraping across the floor as it was dragged away from the curtain in front of their hiding-place, towards the corner. A voice was raised again, threateningly. There was a loud report, followed by a thud, and more scuffling. They could hear the intruder rummaging about the room, opening drawers, throwing things aside. After more searching, there was a cry of frustration, followed by the noise of the bed being kicked and the sound of footsteps leaving the room. They waited and listened in the hope that Old Charvis might give them the all-clear, but there was an ominous silence. The beams of the old house creaked. Billy started moving.

'Not yet,' whispered Titch. 'Not for a bit.'

They waited until the silence became oppressive; then Titch nudged the panel open and began, very tentatively, to crawl out. It seemed safe enough for Billy to emerge too, and they were on the point of coming out into the room when they realised that yet another visitor was mounting the ladder to Charvis's door. Had the intruder come back? It was too late now to retreat: still concealed by the curtain, all they could do was stay

where they were, be as still as possible, and hope. They heard footsteps entering the room – heavier shoes this time, boots maybe.

Through a tear in the curtain, Titch could just see the intruder's waist and shoulders but, frustratingly, could not identify him. He stood in the middle of the room, unmoving, then they heard him make his way back to the door. As he descended the ladder, Titch glimpsed his face, and had to stifle a yelp of fright. Then he was gone. Again, Titch and Billy waited. Eventually, Titch whispered, 'Did you clock who that was, Billy?'

'No. I couldn't see a thing. Did you?'

'Ay.'

'Who?'

'The Creeper.'

'The Creeper! Wow! We should get out, Titch.'

'Let's give it another minute. To be safe.'

When they were certain the coast was clear, they emerged nervously from their hiding-place. What they saw was much worse than anything they could have imagined. The tiny room was in chaos. The bed had been pulled away from under the eaves and pushed to one side. Old Charvis lay, his torso on the floor, his feet on the bed. His arms were splayed wide, and his face was fixed in a look of surprise. He seemed longer and thinner than ever. From underneath his body a slowly growing pool of blood was seeping out into the room. He had been shot in the chest at very close range. Neither Titch nor Billy had ever seen a dead body before. They stood rooted to the spot, staring at the corpse. They didn't hear the footsteps behind them. They didn't hear the ladder creak. They just heard a voice.

'Hoy. You two.'

They nearly fainted from shock. Whipping round, they found themselves face to face with . . .

'Wow!' screamed Billy. 'Sam!'

'Sam! You scared the living daylights out of us.'

'Sorry.'

Titch and Billy were white, trembling.

'Sorry. I was being careful.' Sam was perched on top of the ladder. 'I saw the Creeper leaving in a cab as I came up the street. I didn't know what I was going to find.' Sam manoeuvred his way over the splintered pieces of door and the three of them stood looking at Old Charvis, relieved to be together. 'Thank heavens you're both all right. Did you see who did this?'

'No.'

'We were hiding.'

Sam went over to the body and placed a finger on Charvis's neck. 'No hope, I'm afraid. No pulse at all.'

'This is terrible, Sam,' whispered Titch.

'We should get out,' said Billy.

'I'm thinking.'

'What?'

'I'm thinking.'

'We should get out,' Billy repeated nervously.

'Old Charvis *had* something,' Sam insisted. 'That's what he's been killed *for*.'

'But it's terrible.'

'He had something he was going to give *me*. In return for this.' Sam showed them the envelope in his pocket. 'I've got money for him. And he had something for *me* . . . to give *her*.'

'We should get out, Sam.' Titch was shivering.

'We might get caught.'

'I'm thinking.'

Titch's eyes were fixed on Old Charvis. She had been nursing him. And now he was dead. 'I don't like this, Sam.'

Sam pushed the chair, which had been knocked over, to one side. 'Here give me a hand.' He lifted one corner of the tattered carpet, and indicated to Titch to take the other. Reluctantly, Titch took hold of the frayed edge.

'Come on, Billy. Lend a hand.'

'What's this *for*, Sam?'

'Just pull.'

Together they moved the carpet, which was covered with pieces of paper, opened boxes and clothes ripped from the small chest of drawers. They pulled it as far as they could and let it drop. Instantly, Sam was on his knees, examining the floorboards.

'Ah ha!' He pushed his fingers between the boards. 'Come on, come on,' he urged. He managed to get his fingers underneath the gnarled wood. He raised a small section of flooring and looked down into the space beneath. His face fell. 'There's nothing here.'

'What did you expect?' Titch asked.

'Come on, Sam, we should go.' Billy was edging nervously towards the door.

Sam lay on his side and started feeling around under the floor. 'I don't understand. That night I first came here with Edie, I was sure he had something hidden under here.'

'The police'll be here.'

'Just a minute, Billy.' Sam continued to feel about.

'Sam!'

'I won't be long, Billy.'

'We just want to get out.'

'Go then, Titch.' Sam was straining, exploring every nook and cranny with his arm outstretched beneath the floorboards. 'Wait for me outside.'

'I don't like to leave you.' Titch was white with fear.

'Don't worry. Just go.'

'Come on, Titch. Let's get out,' Billy urged.

Titch turned and stood miserably by the shattered door.

'Hang on,' Sam cried. 'I've got something.' He extricated his arm from under the floorboards. He was holding a small cloth pouch.

'What is it?' Titch asked.

'I tell you what I *think* it is.' He held the pouch up for them to see.

'Not the Rose?'

'No. But something very like it.'

'Let's go! Let's go!'

'Calm down, Billy'

Sam opened the pouch and slid into his open hand two large diamonds, both pinkish in hue. Even in the guttering candlelight and the grim horror of the poky attic they looked startlingly beautiful.

'Wow!'

'Blimey. They're something!'

'We can leave now,' said Sam.

From the door, they looked back at Old Charvis. He lay, sandwiched between the bed and the wall, like a long, thin rag-doll that had been thrown into the corner.

Titch wiped away a tear. 'Just like Edie said.'

'Poor old thing,' said Billy.

'Poor old thing,' said Sam.

And they went.

Safely outside, they sheltered from the snow in the entrance to Farringdon Station.

'Who do you think shot him, Sam?'

'I saw the Creeper just as I got here. That's how I knew there was trouble.'

'The Creeper didn't kill him, Sam.'

'I know that, Billy. Who does the Creeper follow?'

'The Blackbird.'

'Right, Titch. The Blackbird.'

'And you think the Blackbird shot Old Charvis?'

'I do. Yes.'

'But we don't know who the Blackbird is, Sam.'

'I think I do now, but I'm not dead certain. You know the house in Cloak Lane?'

'Where she's staying?'

'Yeah. It's called Broadwaters House.'

'So . . . ?'

'Broadwaters was the name of the Aston's farmstead in South Africa.'

'So . . . ?'

'You remember the Astons had two children?'

'Ay. The daughter's in a mental home.'

'And the son was managing to scrape by, wasn't he –' said Billy, scratching his head, '– hunting expeditions or something?'

'Yeah. Well . . . I think the Blackbird might be him – the son – Edward Aston.'

'Cos Broadwaters House is their London residence, you mean?' asked Titch.

Sam nodded.

'Named after their farm in South Africa?'

'Exactly, Billy.' Sam explained that he would have to pay Broadwaters House another visit in order to confirm the Blackbird's identity.

'It's getting late, Sam.'

'I've got to go anyway, Titch, *she* is expecting me. Listen. While I'm with her, I want you two to persuade Dr Watson to arrange a meeting with Lestrade in the morning. By then I should know for sure about her and the Blackbird.'

Titch and Billy understood Sam's thinking, but Old Charvis's death had brought a note of real danger into their lives. They tried to persuade him not to go, or at the very least not to go alone. Sam was adamant that it would be *more* dangerous if there were two of them.

'But before I go to Broadwaters House, I'm going to take this to the Mr Curtis, the jeweller.' He took out the small jewel pouch and held it up so they could see it clearly. He appeared to take it; then he showed Titch and Billy his empty hand.

'Quit fooling, Sam. This is serious.'

'I know. Sorry. Time to go.'

They covered themselves against the snow and left the shelter of the station. They walked together some of the way, then Sam set out on his own, clutching Old Charvis's jewellery pouch.

'Take care.'

'You too.'

'Bye.'

# 11

# WORKING LATE

R uben Curtis peered through the grimy windowpanes of his shop door and saw Sam, panting on the step. 'Samuel! Come in, come in out of this vile snow.' He opened the door and Sam bounded in. 'Vot on earth do you vont at this hour, my boy? Are you in trouble?'

'I've got something to show you,' said Sam dashing over to the workbench.

'Vot a hurry. Just a moment.' He locked the door and joined Sam, who placed the two diamonds in front of him. He recoiled. '*Oi vey is mir!* Samuel, you *are* in trouble!'

Sam told him Hector's story, and explained how he had come by the two stones. It took some time, but Sam finally persuaded Ruben to look at them.

As Sam had seen him do before, Ruben held the stones under the light at every possible angle. He dismissed the first – 'Schneid, schneid,' – and put it to one side. He pondered long over the second. 'This is quite somethink, Samuel, my boy. If this stone could talk, vot a story it vould tell.' Sam began to wonder if he had perhaps stumbled on the Rose itself. Ruben adjusted his eye-piece, examining in detail the many facets of the stone. He held it to his lip to gauge the temperature. 'Hard to believe it, but this is glass.' Placing it on the workbench, he turned to Sam. 'Vot now, my boy?'

'First thing tomorrow, I am going to tell Inspector Lestrade of Scotland Yard the whole story. In the meantime, would you hold on to these counterfeit stones for me?'

'Are they stolen?'

'No, sir. They don't belong to me, but they are not stolen.'

Ruben grunted disapprovingly. 'For how long do I hold them?'

'There's one thing I have to find out, Mr Curtis.'

'So . . . for how long?'

'Twenty-four hours, sir. Two days at the most. I might even have the answer later tonight.'

'Very vell, Samuel. But I tell you straight – I don't like this.'

At 221b, Billy and Titch explained to Dr Watson what had been happening over the previous two days. Watson was not pleased.

'Did I not make myself clear? You were to wait for Mr Holmes to return.'

'Sam was worried about Hector, Doctor.'

'I know, I know, but I simply don't approve – as you are well aware. And it's *dangerous*!' Watson shook his head. 'Ah well. It's done now. We shall all convene with Inspector Lestrade in the morning as you ask, and see what he can do. Where is our young detective now?'

'He was going to see your jeweller.'

'What?! I can't imagine Mr Curtis will be overpleased to have visitors at this hour of the night. Sam does get carried away rather, doesn't he?'

'Ay, Doctor. He's unstoppable.'

On his earlier visit to Broadwaters House Sam had seen a caped figure in an upstairs window whom he believed to be Edward Aston – the Blackbird. On this visit, he hoped to persuade Irene Adler to confirm the Blackbird's identity, and admit her own. He knew that this was fraught with danger.

From the corner of Cloak Lane, through the snowy night, Sam could just make out the squat figure of the Creeper – Uriah Pogue – back at his post, unmoving in the falling snow. 'If he stays there much longer,' thought Sam, 'he'll look like a snowman.'

To reach the garden wall, Sam walked backwards down the passage – leaving his footsteps the only visible marks in the fresh snow. He hoped this might throw Pogue – should he be alert enough – off the scent. He climbed the wall and dropped into the back garden. The light was on in the piano room. Faintly, he could hear a dulcet voice, and already he felt himself falling under 'the woman's' spell.

Sam rolled up a handful of snow and threw it at the window. The music stopped, and she appeared, shading her eyes to see into the white garden. Spotting Sam she waved. He went and stood by the garden door. Within seconds she was there.

'Sam! Are you all right?'

'Yes thanks, miss.' Kicking the snow off his shoes, Sam went in. She led him downstairs, into the kitchen. As she lit the oil lamp, placing it on the table, she said, 'What have you to tell me that you should be out so late? Sit down. I fear some bad news.'

Sam did as he was told. 'It's not *good* news, I'm afraid, miss.' Deliberately, he placed her envelope on the kitchen table. 'I was unable to give this to Mr Charvis.'

'Why? Was he not there?'

'Not that, miss. Worse than that. I don't like to say.'

'What, Sam? Tell me.'

'He's dead.'

She did not react at all. Then she sat down, opposite Sam. He could now see her face clearly. 'Oh dear,' she breathed. 'Oh dear. That is very awkward.' *Awkward*, thought Sam. A strange response. There was no suggestion that the old boy's death upset her. Nor did she ask *how* he had died. It was almost as though she had expected it. Sam was intrigued by her coldness. He watched, as she gathered her thoughts. She looked quite ravishing in the soft glow of the lamp, and when her pale blue eyes turned to gaze sadly at him, he was hypnotised.

'Are *you* all right, sweet Sam? Has it been very horrible for you?'

'It's not been much fun but I'm fine, thanks, miss.'

'I am very relieved to hear that, my sweet Sam. What would I do without you?' she purred.

'You said that before, miss, when you promised me

an explanation, like . . . you know . . .'

She rose, and moved to the range. 'Would you like some more sweet tea? While I explain?'

'Thank you, miss.'

'Where would you like me to start?'

Sam was astounded – she was trying to find out how much he knew before she committed herself. He took his courage in his hands. 'I think you should go right back, miss . . . to South Africa.'

She paused, not looking at him but concentrating on making the tea. 'As I said before, Sam, for a sweet boy you drive a hard bargain.' She made his tea in complete silence. Sam sensed she was playing for time. When she had finished, she placed it with milk, sugar and a spoon on the table, and sat, almost confrontationally, in front of him. 'Who do you *think* I am?' she asked, implying that whatever Sam thought, he was wrong.

Sam didn't hesitate. 'You're Irene Adler. I've seen a photograph of you. But this was the clincher –' he indicated Old Charvis's envelope, '– same writing as the dedication on your photo.'

Looking up from the envelope, Sam was shocked to see that she had moist eyes. This time, Sam distrusted her tears.

'I have fooled them all, sweet, special Sam, but not

you.' A single tear fell slowly down her cheek. She gazed at him, smiling gently. Her tongue flicked out and licked the tear away. 'I wonder if my poor dead son would have been as clever as you. Give me a moment.'

She had confessed. Sam was pleased. 'That's all right, Miss Adler, I can wait,' he remarked quietly. Again she smiled. Sam put the milk and sugar in his tea and stirred it, while she composed herself.

'I will keep my promise, Sam, and tell you everything,' she said. 'Please, promise me something in return.'

'What?'

'To help me.'

'How?'

'Just help . . . as you have done tonight . . .'

'If I can, miss.' The fact that she wanted Sam to help her, he calculated, might give him some bargaining power, and increase his chances of finding out about the Blackbird.

'Thank you, Sam.' He wondered if she was ever going to tell him her story. Then, eventually, quietly, she began. 'I am alone, I have *been* alone, sweet Sam, since a cruel man betrayed me. I left my husband for him – soft-hearted fool that I am. He used me, in order to become familiar with some dear friends of mine.'

'The Astons, miss?'

She was mildly impressed that Sam had picked up on her story so fast. She went on. 'He used me . . . to steal from them. He took their most precious possession.'

'You mean the Rose of Africa?'

'Yes, Sam. I do.'

'Was it Lord Scarsbury, miss?'

Her look clouded. 'I don't need to tell you anything. You know it all.'

'I don't actually. There's quite a lot I can't work out,' Sam remarked bluntly.

She turned away, as if she were suppressing a smile, then resumed. 'It *was* Lord Scarsbury. When he had the Rose in his grasp, he cast me aside. My friends . . .' – Sam observed that she avoided using the name Aston – 'my friends suffered a great deal. In the wake of the theft, death and madness visited them. I promised the two surviving children I would try and recover their precious Rose for them, and vowed to myself that in the process I would hurt Lord Scarsbury.' Her voice was low and steely. 'I came to London for my revenge, when I heard that Quentin – Lord Scarsbury – had deposited the Rose at the African Diamond Company, and I used Hector – shamelessly, I confess – to gain access to it. Hector made it easy for me, but I did *not* mean to harm him and I am devastated by what has happened. After our bungled attempt to steal the Rose, I had to hide. My pistol – a gift from Quentin – implicated me in the murder.'

Sam sipped his tea. 'I'm interested in your pistol, miss.'

'Are you now?'

'Was it returned to you when it was lifted from Scotland Yard?'

Her brow lowered and she looked at him severely. 'You seem to know an awful lot about . . . about the Rose, Sam.' Her implication – which carried a thinly-veiled threat – was that he knew rather more than was good for him.

'It's for my friend, miss, and his uncle,' Sam said as innocently as he could.

'Yes.' She examined him. 'I see.' He had surprised her, and Sam could see her wondering just how much he did know. 'My pistol, to answer your question, *was* returned. As a matter of fact I have it here, in the pocket of my skirt.' The hair on Sam's neck stood up. He was alone with Irene Adler, a woman everyone had told him was treacherous. Sherlock Holmes thought her capable of murder. She slid her hand into her skirt pocket. 'Would you like to see it?'

Sam's stomach turned over. 'No thanks, miss. I'll take your word for it.' Holding his nerve, he asked, 'Who *took* it from Scotland Yard, miss?'

With her eyes on Sam, and her hand still in her pocket, she replied, 'Some colleagues of Mr Charvis. They knew I was paying him well and tried to blackmail me. They threatened to give me up to the police.'

'I see.' Sam didn't believe her. Her answer was clever but he didn't believe it. He was convinced she was behind the recovery of the pistol from Scotland Yard – she had given money to the two men in the King's Cross wine lodge. Sam decided it would be safer not to pursue this line of questioning. 'Might I have a bit more sugar, please, miss?'

'Help yourself.'

As he did so, Sam's brain was working overtime, trying to figure out how far he could go – how badly she needed his help. And what for. 'Miss Adler, how did the shooting in the African Diamond Company happen?'

'Ah. Something you don't know.' She leaned back and sighed. 'It was a dreadful accident. Hector and I were surprised by the Shift Manager, who was of course

182

very angry. He was *so* angry he was about to strike Hector. I thought the sight of my pistol would stop him – but it enraged him further. He tore it from my hand and threatened me with it.' Her hand moved in her skirt pocket, as if she might be adjusting the position of the pistol. Sam's hackles rose. 'Hector, dear Hector, intervened to defend me. He fought for the gun, and in the scuffle it went off, killing the Shift Manager.' There was something pat about her account of the murder which Sam did not believe. 'I was hysterical,' she continued, 'but Hector took control. He said he would face the consequences alone, and got us out quickly.'

Sam again noticed her use of 'us'! 'When you say *us*, miss, who else was with you?'

She sat forward, a sudden, flustered movement, and looked directly at Sam. 'Did I say *us*? I meant me. We were alone. Just Hector and me.' Sam had always suspected that a third person had been present in the vaults. In spite of her denial, he was certain 'us' had been a slip. 'My escape was so rushed and frantic,' she continued, taking her handkerchief from her sleeve and dabbing her eyes with it, 'I didn't believe Hector would keep his word, but he is a good man.'

Hector had lied to protect Irene Adler. Sam now

suspected that *she* was lying to protect her accomplice, whom he conjectured was the person really responsible for the murder of the Shift Manager. Sam was more and more certain that the accomplice, the murderer, would turn out to be the man in the upstairs window, the Blackbird, Edward Aston.

'What about the Rose, Miss?'

She tensed, and her hand returned to her skirt pocket. 'You are merciless, Sam.'

'I'm sorry, miss, but Hector's been accused of the robbery as well.'

She took a deep breath, then looked straight at Sam. 'The irony is, Sam, that the Rose – the cause of it all –' she shook her head slightly, as if in disbelief at what had happened, '– the Rose was not there. The deposit box was empty. This whole tragedy need never have occurred.'

Practically word for word, this was Hector's story, and Sam hadn't believed it then. 'So where is the Rose now, miss?'

She continued to gaze at him, a look both wry and accusatory. 'Sweet Sam, I wish I knew.'

He wanted to believe her, but again he didn't. 'What does Old Charvis have to do with it, Miss Adler?' Then, correcting himself, 'I mean . . . *did* he have . . .?'

She relaxed back into her chair once more. 'Lord Scarsbury is impossibly wealthy. My plan was to steal the Rose, then sell it back to him. He would have paid almost anything – he has always been obsessed by it. His humiliation – to make him buy back that which he had stolen – would have been glorious, and the money would have restored my friend's fortunes.' Sam felt her story didn't quite add up. 'Mr Charvis was my go-between,' she continued, 'but without the Rose I was lost. He had the idea of a counterfeit – that was the package he should have given you tonight. Without it, I am lost again. And that, sweet Sam, is why I need you.' At last – a hint as to why she needed his help. Sam said nothing and waited. 'If I could get hold of Mr Charvis's package, Sam, I could still implement my plan.'

Finally, Sam knew why she was bothering to answer his questions. 'You want *me* to get it for you,' he stated baldly.

'Do you think that might be possible, Sam?'

As the package was already securely lodged with Ruben Curtis, Sam felt strangely powerful. 'Well, miss. It won't be easy, but I could have a try,' he lied.

'Thank you, sweet Sam. Thank you. You are the only person who can help me . . .'

'But I'm not the only person, am I?' Sam insisted.

'What do you mean?'

'What about the man upstairs?' Sam was still eager to find out about Edward Aston, the Blackbird whom he suspected of being the killer of the Shift Manager. If he was right, and she was lying to protect him, of the many perils he faced alone with Irene Adler in this dimly lit basement kitchen, confirming the Blackbird's identity was the most dangerous.

'What *about* him?' she demanded.

'Please, miss. Who is he?'

'He owns this house. I told you.'

'And what about the man in the cape?'

'Who?'

'The man in the black cape who visited you at Fox Court.'

'Sam!' she cried with indignation. 'I don't know who you mean!'

'You do, miss. You expect me to do things for you and you treat me like a kid.'

Her hand, gripping her handkerchief, hit the kitchen table. 'No!'

Sam was only too aware that her other hand was still in her pocket, holding the pistol. Nervous but determined, he continued. 'There's a man's life at stake here, miss. A man in a black cape visited you in Fox Court. I saw him there! I only want to know who he is.'

She closed her eyes and stroked her forehead with the tips of her fingers. She breathed out, with resignation. The damp handkerchief remained on the table. She looked Sam straight in the eyes. 'The man in the cape is someone who helps me financially.' Sam could see she wanted him to think that the man upstairs and the man in the cape were different people. He didn't dare push her any further, but this deception of hers confirmed in Sam's mind the likelihood that they were one and the same – Edward Aston, the Blackbird. Before he was able to speak, she changed the subject – further proof perhaps. 'I have been desperate, Sam. Please help me.'

'I've already said I'll help you, miss. But can I ask . . . if you testify against Lord Scarsbury, would it be enough to convict him for stealing the Rose from the Astons?'

'It would, Sam,' she smiled. 'And nothing would give me greater pleasure.' That at least had the ring of truth, thought Sam. 'If you help me now, Sam, I will do anything I can for Hector.'

'So . . . if I can get Old Charvis's counterfeit for you . . .'

'You think it possible?'

'You would like me to try and arrange for Lord Scarsbury to buy it back? Correct?'

She nodded. 'My, oh my. You *are* clever, sweet Sam. You will do this for me?'

Sam made her wait before saying, 'Yes, miss. I will.'

She withdrew her hand slowly from her pocket. Sam was relieved to see there was no pistol in it. 'Thank you, thank you.' She stretched her arm out towards him in a gesture of gratitude, not noticing that as she did so, she caught her handkerchief, nudging it into Sam's lap. 'Oh, thank you, sweet Sam.'

Sam looked down, and in the corner of the crumpled lace he could see, delicately embroidered in pink silk, the initials I.A.

# 12

# THE DEAL

The next morning, a day of ice and bitter cold, Sam persuaded Dr Watson to take on the tricky job of dealing with Inspector Lestrade. Watson could not really refuse to help, now that the Irregulars proposed to hand over the active dangers of the case to Scotland Yard.

The Inspector came unwillingly to Baker Street, where Watson regained possession of Holmes's photograph of Irene Adler, and played on Lestrade's guilty conscience. He suggested that if Lestrade implemented Sam's plan, he might make quite a name for himself. Lestrade didn't like being manipulated, but the plan not only held out the possibility of arresting Lord Scarsbury, the original thief of the Rose of Africa, but also the enticing prospect of apprehending the adventuress Irene Adler – something the great Sherlock Holmes had failed to achieve. Sam also predicted that Lestrade would discover who had shot the Shift Manager and Old Charvis, and that he *should* be able to arrest the suspect. The added carrot of recovering the Rose itself was something Lestrade found irresistible, and much as the Inspector was irritated by Sam's cleverness, Lestrade's vanity got the better of him.

Sam remained at Baker Street to talk his plan through in detail with Lestrade and Watson, while Titch, Potts and Edie were despatched to keep an eye on Broadwaters House in Cloak Lane. Billy – in pageboy uniform – went to The Fitzroy to set up a meeting between Lord Scarsbury and Ruben Curtis. When he returned, Sam took him straight to Hatton Garden.

Using the curve of Cloak Lane, Potts, Edie and Titch positioned themselves on either side of Broadwaters House. For cover, Potts and Edie, who were monitoring Irene Adler, were selling matches. Titch, whose task was to keep an eye on the Blackbird, had a brush – to sweep aside the snow for passers-by, although few but the faithful braved the foul conditions on this wintry Sunday. The snow was again falling heavily, coating the ice and frozen sludge with a clean layer of white. After watching for most of the afternoon, Edie asked Potts, 'Why is Uriah Pogue not here, do you think?'

'If 'e's not watchin' the Blackbird, Edie, I deduce, 'e must be watchin' 'is nibs!'

'Lord Scarsbury?'

'Well that's 'oo's payin' 'is bills, innit?'

'Sure. I'm jumpy, Potts. I got a bad feeling.'

'Don't worry, Edie. None of us can get hurt.'

'I wish I was so sure.'

In the small living-room above his shop, Ruben Curtis sat in his rocking-chair squirming with discomfort. As he rocked, the chair squeaked. '*Oi vey*. You two! I am very uneasy about this.'

'There's no need to be, sir,' said Sam.

'Samuel, never in my life have I been involved in anything underhand. Never.'

'But, sir, you're not,' protested Billy. 'You're helping the law.'

'By dealing in schneid jewellery?' Ruben shivered. 'I'm cold. I'm nervous. Ven vill this aristocrat be here?'

'Not till it's dark,' said Sam. 'I'm going now, to make

sure everything else is in order. Billy will stay with you. All right?'

'Not really, Samuel. Vot if this Scarsbury spots it's a fake?'

'Just tell him you're the middle man and *you've* been duped too. But you needn't worry, Mr Curtis, it's a good fake, and he's greedy.'

'He is, Mr Curtis. When I went round to arrange your meeting with him, he was practically dribbling he was so keen. Disgusting.'

'He wants the Rose back, sir, and he wants it bad. You'll do brilliant. Billy, you have to let us know when Scarsbury's about to leave – one candle in the upstairs window if the deal goes through. Mr Curtis, and you, Billy *when* Scarsbury leaves, stay inside. That's when the police will move in. That's when it could get nasty. See you later.'


'Hey, Potts, look, will you?' cried Edie.

The door of Broadwaters House opened, and through it came a man in a black cape.

'The Blackbird!'

'Sure, he's in a hurry.'

'Not 'arf!'

The Blackbird strode to the end of the street,

skidding on the ice. Titch gave Potts and Edie the thumbs-up and set off in pursuit. Potts and Edie resumed their vigil over Miss Irene Adler.

'Tell you wot, Edie, I'll just go check that passage round the back wot Sam mentioned – make sure Miss Adler don't do a bunk that way. Shan't be a mo'. You be all right?'

Edie smiled. She couldn't get used to the idea of Potts taking care of her. 'Sure. I'll be fine. Don't be too long.'

'Keep an eye open for the Doc!'

'Will do. Off you go.'


On top of a hansom-cab, discreetly parked so he could observe Ruben Curtis's shop, Sam was sitting huddled, well wrapped up against the piercing wind and drifting snow. He preferred the cold and the company of the driver to that of Inspector Lestrade, who was in the cab below with Dr Watson. Lestrade sipped from a hip-flask of brandy to keep himself warm.

'Inspector, have you heard from the police in South Africa?'

'Indeed I have, Doctor. They would be more than grateful if Scarsbury could be charged. Their failure to apprehend him at the time caused something of a scandal. But to be frank, I'm uneasy about all this. I dislike being bossed about by Mr Holmes, and this lad Wiggins, really . . .'

'I do understand, Inspector. I have always opposed these children working for Holmes, but I am obliged to admit they do it of their own free will – they seem to enjoy it.'

'But it's when something goes wrong . . .' said Lestrade darkly.

A knock on the cab door broke the doom-laden mood. Watson peered through the small, round, iced-up window.

'Come in, Titch. Quick,' he cried, opening the door. Titch leaped up into the cab, accompanied by a flurry of snow. 'What is it?'

'The Blackbird, sir. He's left Broadwaters House. Took a cab. I couldn't keep up with him, but he's definitely on the move.'

Watson looked to Lestrade who took his watch from his waistcoat pocket. 'Seems a little early.'

'Nevertheless, this is pretty much what Sam predicted, isn't it, Inspector?'

'I suppose so, Doctor,' Lestrade admitted grudgingly. 'I will go and warn my men. I have a constable standing by to go with you when you decide to leave, Doctor. Just give me the word.' So saying, he pulled his coat tight around him, drew his collar up, fixed his hat upon his head and ventured out into the bitter cold.

Now that Lestrade had gone, Sam climbed down into the cab, flexing his frozen joints.

'Hallo, Doctor. Titch says the Blackbird's on the move, eh?'

'Indeed.'

'Good. How were Potts and Edie, Titch?'

'All right, Sam.'

'No movement from Miss Adler?'

'Not yet. No.'

Watson sensed Sam's apprehension. 'Are *you* all right, Sam?'

'Not sure, Doctor. May have bitten off more than I can chew. Lestrade thinks I have.'

'Well he's always wrong, ain't he?' said Titch.

'Let's hope so.'

Watson smiled.

'Hey, look!' said Titch.

They watched as a hansom-cab pulled up in front of Ruben's shop. A squat figure, indistinct in the swirling snow, jumped out mounted the steps and rang the bell.

'That's not Scarsbury!'

'Looks more like Pogue.'

'Pogue! That's not the plan. I hope I haven't got it all wrong.'

'Not you, Sam. Never.'

Watson began putting on his gloves. 'I think perhaps I should take my constable and join Potts and Edie. What do you think, Sam?'

'Maybe, sir. Better safe than sorry.'

'I'll be off then.'

'The door!' cried Ruben Curtis, leaping out of his rocking-chair. 'He's here!'

'Don't worry, sir. I'll go,' said Billy. 'You sit down. *Calm* down.' He descended the narrow stairs fast, ran through the darkened shop and unlocked the door, expecting to see Lord Scarsbury. He was surprised to find himself looking at a squat, dark man with a large moustache. Billy had never seen him before, but, instantly, he knew he was face to face with the Creeper.

'I'm here on behalf of Lord Scarsbury.'

'Your name, sir?' said Billy.

'Pogue. Uriah Pogue.'

This was not what Sam had planned for. 'Is Lord Scarsbury not coming?' Billy asked hesitantly.

'If everything is to my liking, I shall fetch His

Lordship.' Potts's deduction had been correct – Pogue was looking after Scarsbury.

'I see. It's not quite the arrangement, but you'd better come in.' He ushered Pogue into the shop. 'Wait here, please. I'll just warn Mr Curtis.'

Billy wasn't sure how Ruben would take this change of plan. The old man was very jumpy, and Billy was afraid he might give the game away. Upstairs, in the small living-room above the shop Ruben was rocking fretfully to and fro in his chair.

'Don't panic, Mr Curtis,' whispered Billy. 'Don't speak to this bloke. Don't say a thing. He's here to case the joint for Scarsbury, that's all.' Ruben was shaking like a leaf. 'Calm down, sir. I'm going to ask him up. All right?'

Ruben nodded unhappily. When Pogue entered Ruben sat and watched nervously, wringing his hands as Pogue – rudely ignoring Ruben – examined the room. Pogue took his time, burrowing, sniffing like a rodent. When he was satisfied he said, 'You're Mr Curtis, I presume?'

'I am, sir.'

'Upstairs?'

'My bedroom,' replied Ruben.

'May I?'

'If you have to.'

Accompanied by Billy, Pogue completed his detailed search of Ruben's home. Then he confronted the old jeweller. 'Very well, I shall go for Lord Scarsbury. He is expecting you to give him the Rose, Mr Curtis. No messing. Comprendi?' He glanced at the table where a piece of black velvet and a work light waited in readiness. 'If he accepts the authenticity of the jewel, he will pay you with other stones. Not in cash. That's the deal. Understood?'

'Understood,' said Ruben miserably.

'And you, young man . . .' Pogue turned a gimlet eye on Billy, '. . . you let His Lordship *in*. You bring him up *here*. You disappear *upstairs*. Right?' Billy nodded. 'I shall wait in the shop. Afterwards . . . you bring him down to me. By the way, I should warn you both,' Pogue tapped his jacket pocket, 'I am armed.' Ruben and Billy stood frozen. 'Comprendi?'

Ruben let out a low moan.

'Nuffing doin' round the back, Edie. No sign of Pogue. And Miss Adler is singin' – cool as a bloomin' cucumber.' As Potts spoke, Irene Adler rose from the piano and appeared at the front window. She stood looking out into the snowbound darkness of Cloak

Lane, before slowly drawing the curtains.

'Sure, that's a shame.'

'We can't see 'er now.'

'Isn't that why she's doing it?'

'Yeah. How *you* doin', Edie?'

'I'm a bit on the cold side.'

'I bet you are. Look, there's still no sign of the Doc, so why don't you go for a stroll? Warm yerself up a bit. It's not snowing, now.'

'Sure, I wouldn't mind.'

'I'll 'old the fort. Don't go too far.'

'I won't – it's too dark.'


'See this hansom-cab, Titch?' said Sam, rubbing on the icy window.

'Yeah.'

'That'll be Scarsbury.'

'You reckon?'

'Potts would give you odds.' The cab drew up in front of Ruben's shop. With the snow no longer falling, they could make out Pogue opening the cab door for Lord Scarsbury, who was wearing an overcoat with an extravagant fur collar.

'Stone me, Sam.'

'He don't look short of a bob or two, does he?'

The door of Ruben's shop opened – they caught a glimpse of Billy. Lord Scarsbury and Pogue went in. Scarsbury's hansom remained outside the shop.

'Time for the deal,' said Sam.

'Cross your fingers,' said Titch.

Sam took his hands from between his legs, where he was keeping them warm, and held them out to Titch. All his fingers were already crossed. Both hands.

# 13

# THE BLACKBIRD

Billy didn't like Lord Scarsbury. He was a large man, with an angry, reddish face and a square, thrusting jaw. Billy offered to hold his hat, but Scarsbury ignored him, turning to Pogue. 'Upstairs?'

'Yes, sir,' Pogue replied. Scarsbury moved straight to the stairs. 'Get up there, boy,' said Pogue. Billy followed immediately. He passed through the living-room where Scarsbury was already introducing himself to Ruben – there was no doubt who was in charge – and sped up to Ruben's bedroom. The house was so small he could hear the proceedings below quite plainly. Scarsbury's aristocratic tone was brusque, rude.

'Where is it, then?'

'I have your Rose in my safe, Your Lordship,' said Ruben. 'A gem of such quality—'

'Just get on with it,' Scarsbury snapped.

'May I offer you a drink? Somethink to keep out this vile cold?'

'No. Just get the Rose.'

'I shall get it for you. But if in this tone you continue to speak to me, up vill go the price.'

Billy couldn't believe his ears.

'Just get the Rose, Mr Cur—'

'Lord Scarsbury,' Ruben interrupted. 'Never before have I done anythink like this. Only now I do it to help a friend. A common criminal I am not.' Billy's heart was jumping. Ruben was telling Scarsbury in no uncertain terms that he knew he had stolen the Rose from the Astons. He went on, 'For over fifty years have I been a diamond dealer. I handled in my time some exquisite stones, but the jewel of vich ve speak this night is vun of the most beautiful things . . .'

'Mr Curtis—'

'It is not somethink over vich to rush. Vot to you is just a possession, to me is vun of nature's miracles. Please to take off your things. Make yourself at home in my humble house, and take a glass of vodka vith me. Vile this you think about, from the safe I vill get the stone.'

Billy was in a cold sweat. He could hear Ruben going

down to the workshop. Left alone, Scarsbury was cursing under his breath, but when Ruben returned he had removed his hat and coat. He was obliged to wait while the old man poured the drinks, the bottle chattering nervously against the glasses.

'Lord Scarsbury, to meet you is an honour, even in these questionable circumstances. Vith me, to drink together before ve deal, is tradition, and this toast was beloved of my father . . .

'Ve come into life naked and bare.
Ve go through life vith trouble and care.
Ven ve leave this life ve go *God* knows vere!
But if ve're all right here, ve'll be all right there.
*Lechayim* – vich means – To life!'

Billy heard the chink of glasses. The atmosphere was warmer, but remained tense. Ruben's nerves were settling. He lit the lamp, smoothed the black velvet and sat, opposite Scarsbury. On the velvet he positioned a small, round convex mirror. He produced a pouch and, with hands trembling slightly, slid . . . on to the mirror . . . into the pool of light . . . Old Charvis's schneid Rose. The light and mirror were so cunningly arranged that the room was suffused with a pink glow, which seemed to emanate from the stone itself.

'There. A thing of awe, Your Lordship. Such beauty is rare.' Ruben looked up at Scarsbury through his thick glasses. Scarsbury's gaze was fixed on the stone. He inhaled deeply, slowly. He relaxed. He almost smiled.

'I always wanted it, Mr Curtis. Always. I don't know why.'

'Our deepest desires are not rational.'

'I would have done anything to get it back. Anything.'

Ruben was surprised, impressed by his openness. 'Please to take a closer look – here.' He handed Lord Scarsbury a pair of large tweezers. Scarsbury ignored them and picked up the fake jewel. 'And there, if you wish,' said Ruben with a tinge of panic, 'is my loupe.'

'Eh?' Scarsbury grunted.

'My eye-piece.'

Scarsbury picked up the loupe. He held the jewel and scrutinised it lovingly. This was the most dangerous moment of the negotiation. Billy sensed what was happening, and, like Ruben, he held his breath.

Scarsbury turned the schneid jewel this way and that. Ruben sat, his heart racing, awaiting the verdict.

He sensed that Scarsbury was not that knowledgeable about diamonds, and, as he had just confessed, he wanted this stone very badly. He removed the eyeglass and placed the diamond back on the mirror. He did not speak. Ruben waited. Was Scarsbury going to accept it? Had he seen through it?

'Truly,' said Ruben, fighting to conceal his nerves, 'it is an honour to handle such a quality gem. You must be very relieved, sir, to have it back after all this recent . . . er . . . fuss and nonsense, shall ve call it?'

'I *am* relieved,' said Scarsbury, still gazing at the diamond. 'I truly am.' But still he did not give his verdict.

'Vell . . . shall ve perhaps look now at vot for me you have? Yes?' Still Scarsbury did not reply. 'If you are content.'

'Yes,' said Scarsbury. 'Yes. Let us move on.'

Billy breathed a sigh of relief. The change in Scarsbury was so swift, Ruben was slightly suspicious. From being mistrustful and bullying, he had become compliant, even gentle. Scarsbury leaned across to his coat and from the pocket took out a bag of jewels which he placed on the table.

Ruben moved the fake Rose on its mirror respectfully to one side, undid the tie on the bag, and on to the black velvet poured rubies, amethyst, emeralds, opal – a stream of precious gems.

'*Oi vey!*' He pushed his thick-lensed glasses up into the grey hair on his forehead and picked up his eyeglass. 'Vould Your Lordship like another drink vile at these I look?'

'Thank you, Mr Curtis. That would be most welcome.'

'Help yourself. I shall vork as fast as I can.'

'This is taking for ever,' said Sam. 'I'll go mad.'

'At least he ain't come storming out,' said Titch comfortingly.

'True. No news is good news.'

'Well, at least it's not bad news. No sign of the Blackbird, though.'

'He's here already, Titch. He has to be. You saw him leave Broadwaters House.'

'I can't see him now, though.'

'If he shows his hand too soon, they'll get him.'

'Are you sure you're right about who the Blackbird is?'

'I told you when I first went to Cloak Lane, I noticed the name Broadwaters House.'

'The name of the Astons' farmstead in South Africa. I remember.'

'There was also this painting of a river and a place called Tanga-Tanga, and that was where the Astons first found diamonds on their land. It has to be the Astons' London home. On the hatstand there was a black cape, which disappeared, like somebody wanted to hide it. Then I saw this man in an upstairs room. In a cape. Later, I asked Irene Adler who he was and she dodged round it. Who *can* it be? Mum and Dad Aston died.'

'The sister is in a mental home.'

'That leaves the son – Edward Aston. In the papers he comes across as a real wild card, you know – liked his hunting and his guns. He hates Scarsbury and wants revenge – he tried to kill him at the club. What did the gunman say before he fired?'

'*You know what this is for.*'

'Right. So there's some real history there.'

'Ay.'

'So the Blackbird is Edward Aston. Has to be.'

'You're amazing.'

'*If* I'm right, Titch, I'm banking that he'll take another pop at Scarsbury tonight. If he doesn't, I'm stuffed.' They peered out of the cab window again, but nothing was happening; just the gusting wind, disturbing the newly-fallen snow. 'Titch. You know we've always felt that there was a third person in the vaults with Hector and Miss Adler?'

'Ay.'

'I think it was him – Edward Aston. I think *he* shot the Shift Manager. And Old Charvis.'

'Irene Adler's dangerous as well though, Sam. If Mr Holmes couldn't catch her, what chance do *you* stand?'

'I think I know what she'll do now.'

'You're at it again.'

'I know. I can't help it. Sorry.'

Titch couldn't be cross with him. 'What d'you reckon she'll do, then? Run for it?'

'Well . . . that's what I've planned for her to do. If she's got the Rose, she will, won't she? That's why I've got Potts, Edie and the Doc watching her.'

'Ay. And if she hasn't?'

'Lestrade will have the last laugh.'

'We don't want that, do we?'

'Not likely. I'd never live it down. I wish something would bloomin' happen.'

'Ay. It's going on, ain't it?'


Ruben went painstakingly through the jewels one by one. Some he spent little time on. Some he examined in great detail. He muttered frequently under his breath, although Scarsbury could not make out the words: he was getting tense again, and clearly wanted the whole thing to be over. To relieve his anxiety he asked Ruben, 'How did you come by the Rose, Mr Curtis?'

'A colleague asked vould I, for a lady, do a favour.'

Scarsbury's eyes narrowed. 'Did you meet the lady in question?'

'No, sir. Don't even know her name.' Ruben concentrated extra hard on the ruby he was examining.

Scarsbury lapsed into a fidgety silence, glancing anxiously at the schneid Rose as if he longed to pick it up. Noticing this, Ruben remarked, 'It von't run avay, Your Lordship. Not this time.'

Scarsbury was not amused, but Ruben refused to be hurried. Eventually he put down his eyeglass and lowered his spectacles on to his nose.

'Vell, Your Lordship, ve have a deal. Give me please your hand.' Scarsbury took Ruben's hand. 'I think my colleague vill be vell pleased. And you have back your treasured Rose, eh?'

Billy, who was listening intently, lit and placed a candle in the bedroom window – the sign to Lestrade that the deal had gone through and Scarsbury would be leaving shortly. Billy heard him say, 'Thank you,

Mr Curtis.' Then Ruben summoned him.

'Coming, sir.' He ran down the stairs, saw Ruben helping Scarsbury into his fur-collared coat, and continued to the shop below, where Pogue was waiting.

'Check the door, sonny.'

Billy unbolted and unlocked the door, and looked out into the snow.

'All clear, sir. Cab here. Quite safe for Lord Scarsbury to come down.'

'Go and get him then.'

As he crossed to the door, Pogue's hand moved towards the gun in his pocket. Billy shot back up to the living-room and reported, 'All clear.'

Scarsbury turned to Ruben. 'Mr Curtis. I was not looking forward to this and you have made it – almost a pleasure. Goodbye.' Ruben looked as though he was about to pass out with relief. Scarsbury then began to manoeuvre his considerable bulk down the narrow stairs.

Dr Watson had joined Potts and Edie. They were all sitting in a hansom positioned so that they could observe the front door of Broadwaters House. The constable who had accompanied Watson stood guard outside the cab.

'I wonder 'ow the jeweller's gettin' on,' said Potts.

'We shall not know till much later, I suspect,' replied the Doctor.

'Sure,' Edie replied, 'I hope no one gets hurt.'

'Bit bloomin' quiet 'ere, innit?'

Edie nodded. '*Too* quiet, if you ask me. I'm shaking.'

'I'll 'op out. Do the rounds again. You stay warm.'

'Good lad, Potts,' said Dr Watson.

'Shan't be a sec.' Potts leaped from the cab and disappeared up Cloak Lane.

'Can I help, Edie?'

'No thanks, Doctor. It's not the cold, I'm nervous. I just think something terrible is about to happen.'


Outside Ruben's shop, Lestrade and his men were standing by, out of sight, ready to arrest Scarsbury. Sam, waiting with Titch in the cab, was perturbed.

'Still no sign of the Blackbird, Titch.'

'Like you said, Sam, he can't show too soon. Look!' Titch pointed towards the shop. 'The door's opening.'

'Can you see Billy? I'm so wound up I can't watch.'

'Ay.'

'I told him and Ruben not to come out.'

'They're not,' said Titch. 'Pogue is. Billy's inside with Scarsbury. I can't see Mr Curtis at all.'

Pogue carefully examined the interior of the waiting

hansom: he did not want a repetition of events at the club. 'All clear, Your Lordship,' he called.

Scarsbury appeared in the doorway, and as he came down the steps, Billy closed the shop door.

'Come on, Titch,' said Sam. 'We might as well be there for the arrest. Nothing's going to happen now. Blast!' Sam and Titch jumped out of the cab, and began walking across the icy road.

As Scarsbury was crossing the pavement, with Pogue in attendance, the hansom-cab driver rose to his feet, a huge caped figure towering over them on the top of the cab.

'Lord Scarsbury,' he shouted.

Scarsbury stopped dead in his tracks, fear etched into his face.

'Titch!' shouted Sam. 'Keep back – there'll be shooting.'

'What?'

'There'll be shooting. Come back quick. The cabby – it's the Blackbird!'

# 14

# BLOOD IN THE SNOW

The Blackbird looked enormous, standing on top of the hansom-cab. As Sam and Titch doubled back, taking cover behind their cab on the other side of the road, they could hear him snarling, 'You won't get away with it this time, Scarsbury, you filthy thief!'

Scarsbury was backing towards the shop, whimpering. He slipped and fell, scrabbling up the icy steps. Pogue, gun in hand, was helping Scarsbury to his feet when, from beneath his cape, the Blackbird produced his own weapon. Lestrade, with several of his men, leaped from the shadows, shouting, 'Don't shoot. Do NOT shoot.' But before they could prevent him, the Blackbird fired twice. Scarsbury fell back on to the ice screaming. The police scattered and took cover.

Almost simultaneously Pogue's shot rang out, hitting the Blackbird, who screamed and clutched his chest. His gun fell from his hand, slid off the roof of the cab and plunged noiselessly into a mound of snow. He stood swaying, pointing, yelling desperately, 'May you die in hell, Scarsbury!!! That's for my father! My mother! My sister!' His last words were muffled by the sound of blood gurgling in his throat. Still pointing a finger at Scarsbury, he stood silent for a moment before falling forward, plummeting to the ground, roaring through his pain, 'You evil—' His words were cut off as he hit the ground with an icy crunch. All the breath was dashed from his body, and he lay, moaning, a steady trickle of blood seeping from his chest. Close to him was Scarsbury, writhing in agony – one of the bullets had entered his groin and shattered the pelvis.

Pogue had feared just such another attempt on Scarsbury's life, but had been stunned by the direction from which it had come. He had at least prevented the Blackbird firing more shots, and although Scarsbury was injured, his wounds were not fatal. From all angles, people were now converging on the two wounded men. Lestrade was the first to arrive. He went straight to the Blackbird, turning him gently on to his back to examine the bullet wound in his chest.

'This doesn't look good,' he muttered under his breath, then called to his men, 'How is Lord Scarsbury?'

Pogue answered. 'He needs a doctor, Inspector. Fast.'

Lestrade addressed one of his men. 'Get him to hospital.' He turned back to Sam who had his finger on the Blackbird's neck.

'The carotid pulse is almost non-existent, Inspector. We *must* get a confession from him. Quickly. Please.' Sam leaned close to the dying man. 'Mr Aston?'

In reply, Aston moaned. Lestrade was annoyed, although he recognised the need for a confession. Pushing Sam to one side, he knelt beside the Blackbird and heaved his body on to his thighs. He cradled him, his mouth very close to the man's ear.

'Mr Aston, sir, my name is Inspector Lestrade. Mr Aston . . . can you hear me?'

Aston moaned again and nodded his head – cutting off his movement with a yelp of pain.

'Mr Aston—'

'Inspector . . . I . . .' Aston's words were barely audible.

'Mr Aston, is there anything . . .'

'Yes,' spluttered Aston. 'I hope Scarsbury dies, but I am sorry . . .' he was struggling for breath, 'sorry for that fool . . .' Aston's eyes – naive and pleading –

looked up at Lestrade like a child gazing at its mother, an innocence at odds with the words coming from his lips. 'That fool . . . Charvis – he . . . he was cheating us . . . so, I . . . I shot him.' His eyes clouded over and his voice faded to nothing. His body went limp.

'Oh no!' cried Sam. 'We need to know about the Shift Manager! For Hector.'

'Too late, I fear,' said Lestrade.

'Please try again, sir. Please.'

'Wiggins!' cried Lestrade in frustration. Leaning close to Aston's ear again, he whispered, 'Mr Aston. Can you hear me, Mr Aston?'

Aston lay lifeless in Lestrade's arms. Lestrade tried one last time. 'Mr Aston, can you hear me? Mr Aston, did you have anything to do with the shooting of the Shift Manager in the diamond vaults? Were you there? Mr Aston!' Aston did not respond. Lestrade looked up. 'I'm sorry, Wiggins. It's too late.' Sam was distraught. Everything they had done was to prove Hector innocent, and they had been thwarted.

To their surprise, Aston stirred, pulling Lestrade closer to him. His words – spoken with great effort, one or two at a time – were only just comprehensible. 'That deed . . . sits heavily . . . on my conscience, Inspector. Interfering buffoon. He . . . he tried to stop us . . . taking the Rose . . . *our* Rose . . . there was a fight . . .' Aston's body again went limp. This time they thought he really was dead, but then, his lips barely moving, he said, 'I . . . I killed him. It was me, not Irene . . .' His hold on Lestrade slackened, his arm fell, and his body slumped. This time there was no doubt. He slithered from Lestrade's knees on to the icy ground.

Lestrade got up, and, together with Sam and Titch, stood looking down at the lifeless body of Edward Aston, the Blackbird. Scarsbury had been stretchered away, and as Lestrade's men moved in to deal with Aston's corpse, Lestrade turned to Sam.

'Perhaps you see now that this business is not a game, Wiggins. Still, I suppose a kind of justice has been done. Let's get you up to Pentonville – tell your Mr Potts he's off the hook. Dr Watson is due to meet us there later. Isn't that the plan?'

'Yes, Inspector,' said Sam. 'Thank you.'

'Thank you, Mr Lestrade,' said Titch.

'Come on, then.'

'Would it be all right if we had a word with Mr Curtis first, sir?'

'Certainly. Come and find me when you're ready. I've got things to do here.'

They moved towards Ruben's shop and rang the bell. Almost immediately Billy opened the door. Ruben was with him.

'Oi vey! Oi vey! Ve heard the shootink. Thank God you are both vell.'

The four of them stood looking at the spot where, minutes before, Scarsbury had lain wounded, and Aston had died. Stunned by the fatal deeds that had unfolded so swiftly on the pavement below them, they gazed down speechless at the two large bloodstains in the snow.

Unaware of the violent events that had unfolded outside Ruben's shop, Dr Watson sat with Edie in their hansom-cab, waiting for any sign of Irene Adler. Watson was so concerned about Edie that he had removed his own travelling rug and wrapped her in it. But nothing could stop her shaking. Potts had gone to check that Miss Adler was not escaping from the back of the house. Edie murmured that he had been gone too long, repeating her conviction that something terrible was still about to happen. Watson had developed the greatest respect for her 'visions', and was in fact recording them in his private journal. He wrapped Edie tighter in the rug, and rubbed her arms to try and warm her. He did not feel that at the moment there was very much that *could* go wrong – certainly with Potts – who was simply checking the passage behind the house.

Potts was equally chipper as he laboured through the snow, which came up to his knees. He worked his way along the garden wall behind Broadwaters House. The passage was deserted. Indeed, the only thing to cause him any concern at all was that the house was now completely dark – all the lights had been extinguished. It seemed a little early for Miss Adler to retire to bed, but she had certainly not left by the front door, and there were no new footsteps in the snow, so Potts trudged on. He was nearing the end of the passage, where it narrowed before emerging into the road, when he thought he heard a noise behind him.

Spinning round, Potts saw that a portmanteau had been thrown over the wall from the garden of Broadwaters House, landing almost silently in the deep snow. Potts flattened himself against the side of the passage and held his breath. He observed a man jumping from the top of the wall. The man gathered up the bag and began making his way, as hastily as the conditions would allow, in Potts's direction.

The last time Potts had seen Irene Adler, as she closed the front curtains less than an hour before, she had looked beautiful, feminine and elegant. It took Potts a moment to realise that this was probably her – it made sense that, to make her escape, she had changed into male attire. Potts was staggered by the transformation. The man was too busy dusting snow off his bag to notice Potts immediately, but he was getting closer and there was nowhere for Potts to hide. He was trapped. He had to think fast – the man was almost on him. Before he could make up his mind, Potts had been spotted. The man stopped, startled and angry.

'Who are you?' The voice was deep and throaty. Potts was confused as well as shaken. *Was* this Irene Adler? He was unsure. 'What are you doing here?' came again the stern, threatening voice.

'I'm tired, mister,' said Potts defensively, trying to yawn. 'I was just 'avin' a rest out the wind.'

'Get out of my way.'

Potts didn't know what to do for the best. If he let the man pass and ran to alert Dr Watson and the constable, he might lose the trail. The angry figure was elbowing past him. Potts's time was running out. In sudden desperation he said, 'Give us a penny and I'll carry your bag for you?'

'What?' Swiftly, nervously the man drew the bag close to his side, wrapping his arms around it. Potts guessed there was something in it of great importance. The man turned, and light from the one gas lamp in the passage, reflecting in the snow, lit up his face. Potts had seen Irene Adler wearing male disguise in the wine lodge at King's Cross. Seeing again the pencil moustache, he was now certain it was her, but he was so staggered by her skill, so captivated by her performance, that he made a fatal blunder. 'I just asked if I could carry your bag for you, miss?' Miss! The word was spoken. Potts could not take it back.

A hand took him by the throat, and pinned him to the wall. 'Did you say miss, boy?' Potts was gasping, gagging. He could not have replied if he had wanted to. He could not believe he had made such a foolish error, and he feared it might cost him his life. He caught a whiff of violets – a woman's scent, a delicacy at odds with the strength of his attacker. The grip of the hand around his windpipe was ferocious. His head was in a whirl. He remembered Sherlock Holmes's warning that Irene Adler was capable of cold-blooded murder. Before he could heave another breath, he was looking down the barrel of a small pistol; he could not see but his instinct told him that it had a pearl handle, on which were engraved the letters I.A. 'Who *are* you?' growled the voice. The grip on his throat loosened and the pistol was pushed into his chest – 'What are you doing here?' – harder with each question. 'Who sent you? Answer me.' Still breathless, but able at last to speak, Potts proclaimed his innocence, but it was too late.

'Who ARE you, boy? If you want to live, tell me.'

Again Potts protested, but a brutal thrust on the pistol was accompanied by a sharp slap to his face, which stung fiercely in the cold. Again, oddly, he smelled violets. The pistol was taken out of Potts's chest and held before his eyes. 'If you weren't a kid you'd be dead already. Unless you give me a good explanation, boy . . . you leave me no option . . . Tell me who you are. I shall give you five.' Potts was petrified. The count began. 'Five . . . four . . .'

'I don't know what you want me to say . . .'

'Three . . .'

'I ain't done nuffing . . .'

'Two . . .'

'Please . . .' Potts begged, 'please don't shoot me.' He fell to his knees, pleading.

'One . . .'

'I'm sorry, miss!' Again, in his panic, Potts uttered

224

that fatal word. In response, the pistol was jammed under his ribs and pointed directly at his heart. He closed his eyes, held his hands out to protect himself, and waited for the killing shot to ring out in the narrow confines of the passage. He heard the deafening retort of the gun, and almost fainted with shock, but he felt nothing. Was this what it was like to die? He waited for the pain. Nothing happened. Gingerly, in disbelief, he opened his eyes, and saw his attacker gripping a hand, from which blood was dripping. It spattered on to the pistol, which now lay between them in the reddening snow. Potts could smell cordite. Who had fired the shot that had saved him? In the opening of the passage, only a few yards away, he could see the silhouette of a man, smoke rising from his revolver. It was too tall to be Uriah Pogue. Not thin enough to be Sherlock Holmes. To Potts's relief, he realised it was Dr Watson. He half ran, half crawled through the snow and grabbed Watson's leg, hiding behind it to look back on the wounded figure, who was leaning against the wall in pain, staring furiously, longingly, at the pistol, which lay so temptingly close by.

'I shouldn't touch it, if I were you,' said Watson. With his eyes still fixed on Potts's assailant, Watson leaned towards Potts, who was clinging to his leg. 'Are you in one piece, Potts, my lad?'

'Yes, sir, Doctor. Just. Fank you.'

'Run round the corner and find our constable. Bring him here as fast as you possibly can.' Potts scampered off with relief. Watson, keeping his trusty service revolver firmly aimed at Potts's attacker, almost smiled as he said, 'So . . . we meet again . . . Miss Irene Adler.'

# 15

# POPPYCOCK

Leaving Pentonville Prison on his way to Soho, Dr Watson considered the case of Hector Potts. Watson had visited Hector's bedside, and, although he was still weak after the poison attempt on his life, he had been cheered by Watson's news, because he no longer faced the threat of the gallows. Nevertheless, poor, love-stricken Hector felt very foolish – to be seen so publicly to be Irene Adler's dupe, when he had been prepared to die to protect her and her accomplice, Edward Aston. As the case had been brought to a successful conclusion, Watson hoped to persuade Lestrade not to pursue charges of perverting the course of justice, in which case Hector could look forward to the prospect of returning home as soon as he was well enough.

Watson walked down Berwick Street as nimbly as the ice would allow – the pavements had been cleared, but underfoot it was still treacherous. He was perturbed: he was more impressed with Sam and the Irregulars than he cared to admit, but he felt a certain guilt that he had to an extent aided and abetted them in the case of the Rose, and he nursed increasing concerns for their future as members of Holmes's irregular police force.

The Silken Garter was, of course, closed at this hour of the morning, but Mrs Potts ushered Watson into the bar, where he found Potts with his dad, in uniform, Sam and Titch, Billy and Edie. This gathering was supposed to be celebratory, but the atmosphere was somewhat muted. Although officially all the ends of the case had been tied up, questions still hung in the air about Hector's fate, and Irene Adler was not yet behind bars because she was being treated for injuries sustained in the shooting. In addition, they were all saddened by the death of Old Charvis. Both Sam and Potts had had narrow escapes – Potts was lucky to be alive! Had it not been for Watson's own intervention – prompted by Edie – who knows what would have happened?

Watson observed the small team: they were

unusually fractured, preoccupied. Edie had fully recovered – as she always did when her 'visions' had passed – but she had been very frightened by Potts's brush with death, and she was sitting holding his arm. Billy was looking forward to Holmes being back, and was good-humoured as usual – Watson liked him more and more – his heroism in the case of the Dragon Tattoo had been the making of him. Titch was relieved that Sam had survived his encounters with Irene Adler, of whom she had grown rather jealous. Watson thought Titch was sitting, somewhat possessively, rather too close to Sam. Her fondness for him was blatant. He watched the irregulars as they sat, chatting brokenly about the whole affair and wondered what their view of Titch was.

'It's the sister I feel sorry for.' Titch was referring to the younger sister of Edward Aston. She would now be the sole inheritor of the Rose – which had been recovered from Irene Adler's portmanteau – but she was in a mental institution in South Africa. How much she would understand of what had happened, or how much she would benefit from the Rose being returned to her was hard to gauge – it seemed a melancholy outcome for so much risk and effort.

'Wot I don't get is why Aston duffed Old Charvis up.'

'Well, Potts, when I told Miss Adler the old boy was dead,' Sam replied, 'she didn't turn a hair – like she half expected it. I think there was a disagreement between her and Aston – over the counterfeit. Listen. They already had the Rose – thanks to Hector. They could have just flogged it back to Scarsbury. They didn't *need* Charvis's counterfeit – it was an extra – greed on her part, because if she could get Scarsbury to buy the fake Rose, the *real* one could go to the Astons, and she could hang on to the proceeds of the sale. Right? Aston was losing patience. With her *and* Charvis! He thought Charvis was cheating them. He just wanted revenge on Scarsbury. And fast. So he knocked the old boy about to make him get a move on.'

'It worked, didn't it?' observed Titch sadly.

'Sure, I think he was off his chump too, like his poor sister,' Edie chimed in. 'Shooting Scarsbury outside The Fitzroy, beating up dear old Mr Charvis and then killing him – he was losing the plot.'

There was general agreement. Billy then enquired why Irene Adler had gone to The Fitzroy on the night of the shooting. 'That night you followed her, Titch. Why would Irene Adler want to kill Scarsbury? Her whole plan would have fallen apart if he was dead.'

'She wasn't shooting at Scarsbury,' Sam replied.

'What?'

'She was shooting at the Blackbird – Aston – to get him out of the way. He was becoming a liability. And the circumstances that night were perfect.'

'Wow!' Billy couldn't believe a woman was capable of such behaviour. 'She was shooting the man she was in league with?'

'I reckon.'

'She's some dame, isn't she?!'

'When we set out to find the flippin' bird, we never reckoned on one as bad as 'er!'

'La Belle Dame. Sure, what did I say?'

'Wiv no mercy! Spot on, Edie.' Then Potts suddenly asked, 'Hey! Wot's 'appened to the fakes?'

'Well, Scarsbury bought the good one,' said Billy, 'so Lestrade'll have that. Mr Curtis probably still has the other.'

Sam couldn't believe he hadn't thought of that. 'We'd better get it off him as quick as we can. He'll have a heart attack!'

'He was fantastic with Scarsbury. You should have heard him! He was nervous before, but when Scarsbury was rude to him . . . Wow!' Billy recounted Ruben's putting Scarsbury in his place. It was the first time any of them had smiled for some time.

'The uvver fing I don't get, Sam, is 'ow you always knew Irene Adler 'ad the Rose.'

'Titch and I talked it through a lot, didn't we, Titch?'

'Ay. We reckoned that if the Rose hadn't been in the vaults, which was what Hector always claimed . . .'

'A lie, which Irene Adler repeated to me almost word for word . . .' Sam interjected.

'. . . The Shift Manager wouldn't have provoked the shooting.'

'He would have been preoccupied by the Rose being missing,' Sam continued.

'Ay. Hector and Miss Adler were lying. The Rose had to be there. *They* had it. Them and the Blackbird.'

'The Shift Manager was shot because they were stealing it,' Sam concluded. 'No other reason.'

'Ill-fated thing,' added Edie glumly. 'We should get that counterfeit off Mr Curtis before anything else goes wrong!'

'You're right, Edie. I'll pop round and see him straight after this,' said Sam.

'You're dead smart at this deductive stuff, Sam,' observed Potts's dad. 'We could do with chaps like you at Scotland Yard.'

'I believe Sam is rather keen on a career in medicine,

Mr Potts,' intervened Dr Watson. 'That's right, isn't it, Sam?'

'Can't see it happening,' Sam muttered. He was embarrassed to have his future discussed in front of his friends.

'Have faith,' said the Doctor amiably. 'When you're the right age, you can come and work for me at the surgery. And by the way, I think I've found a boat for Titch.'

'Fantastic!' cried Titch.

'I received a letter this morning from the Wapping Punt and Dinghy Company. They have just the thing! In fact,' said the Doctor, 'if you'd like to go and see it now, we could.'

Titch was keen. Sam said he would go and see Ruben. Edie thought it time for her to get to work, and Potts was looking forward to a busy afternoon running for Jacky Dyke. Billy was going for lessons with Watson's friend who was training him to work in a hotel.

'Before you go,' said Lily Potts, 'I know we're all a bit down, but I've got to say, on behalf of my silly brother-in-law, Hector, how grateful we are to you for what you've done. If it wasn't for you lot, he might well be going to the gallows. And Jem and I' – she put a hand on Mr Potts's arm – 'want you to know what a wonderful thing you've done. Thank you.'

'Yes. Thank you,' added Mr Jeremiah Potts.

'And another thing,' Lily said, 'I think you're all very lucky to have the Doctor as a friend. There aren't many kids like you who could look to such a fine man for help and support.'

Watson blushed. 'That's very kind of you, Lily – may I call you Lily?'

'Of course, Doctor!'

'The only one I don't need to help is your son. Potts is lucky. He has you!'

''E wouldn't have had no one at all if you weren't a crack shot, Doctor!' said Mr Potts.

'Dead right, pal! And 'oo knows, Dr W, fings may change! When Billy's got all 'is 'otel savvy under 'is belt, you can buy us that empty building in Baker Street just down from 221b – that'd make the most amazin' 'otel. It'd be the first of a chain of London 'otels wot I would own and Billy would run – specialising in rooms wot ordinary people can afford. Potts and Chizzell – pioneers in workin'-class 'otelery – or wotever you call it! Each 'otel supplied wiv drinkin' water in bottles courtesy of Mr McArdle – Edie's dad and I are going into business togevver to provide our customers wiv safe drinkin' water!' Trust Potts. It didn't take much to make him larky. 'We shall 'ave the beautiful Miss McArdle on the front desk, charmin' the customers.' Edie was tickled pink. 'Titch can take them on boat trips down to 'Ampton Court in one of 'is fleet of fancy barges, and Sam'll be the 'otel doctor . . . "On call, ladies and gentlemen, for your 'ealth and security, at any hour of the day or night!" We'd make a flippin' fortune!'

'You're off the wall, my darling boy,' said Lily, flushing with pride.

'I 'ope so, Mum! I do me best. But listen, I ain't finished. In our 'otels, we can 'ave posh suites for the nobs, and they will all be named after the Irregulars' most famous cases! Eh? The Dragon Suite – that could be done up all Chinesey like, black and gold, dead fashionable. The Irene Adler Suite. On the door there could be this brass plate wiv – wot was that French phrase you used, Edie?'

'La Belle Dame, Potts?'

'That's it! The "La Belle Dame Suite" – all pink diamonds wiv a pianner in! And a reproduction of 'er photo, eh? Wot d'you fink?'

'Sam'd never get to sleep in there, would you?' quipped Titch.

236

Edie grinned. 'Sure, if he did drop off, he might have *nice* dreams instead of nightmares.'

'Wouldn't stop him thinking though, would it?' cried Billy.

Sam put his chin on his hand. 'I've *been* thinking, actually . . .' Before he could finish, the Irregulars drowned him out, roaring with laughter.

'You, Sam?'

'Surely not!'

'Get on!'

Even Sam was obliged to smile. But then he said, 'Seriously though, you lot, Titch and I done a bit of research, and you know what today is? It's Dr Watson's birthday!'

'Why didn't you tell us, Dr Watson?'

''Appy birthday, Doc!'

'Happy birthday, Doctor,' they chorused.

Lily Potts ran to the piano. Edie took Watson by the hand, and they gathered round for a hearty rendition of 'For he's a jolly good fellow!' Sam and Titch shook Watson's hand. Potts and Billy thumped him affectionately on the back. Edie gave him a kiss on the cheek. There was a huge outpouring of affection for the embarrassed Doctor, who could not now *stop* blushing.

When the song was over, Potts observed, 'Trouble is

though, Sam, we ain't got 'im no present.'

'Well actually, we have.'

'Wot!'

'The thing is, it's not here. Mrs Hudson's got it.'

'Wot use is that?'

'Sure, he'll just have to have it later, won't you, Doctor.'

'It will be something to look forward to,' beamed Watson. 'Thank you. Thank you, all. You've become like a family to me! Coming as it does at the end of this dangerous business – and being here with you all – means that this is one birthday I shall never forget! Never! Come on, Lily. Let's have another song!'

Back in their hideout later, Sam and Titch were able to relax together for the first time in days.

'I'm glad this case is over, Sam. It's been weird. Bit nasty.'

'I know, Titch. I'm sorry. I got taken in by the Belle Dame. She sort of put a spell on me, and felt like my mum, all at the same time. I ain't seen my mum in years.'

'Me neither,' said Titch flatly.

They both thought about their mothers.

'Do you miss your mum, Titch?'

Titch considered this for a moment. 'Never really had a mum *to* miss. This is home, now. What about you?'

'I miss my dad. Even though he's been dead for a long time. I think my mum was stupid to hitch up with that horrible beadle, but I don't miss her now. You're my family, Titch. You. The others. Dr Watson.'

'We owe him a lot, don't we? My boat.'

'Everything really, Titch.'

'What do you reckon to this idea of you working for him?'

'Really exciting. I love the books he gives me, but there's a limit to what I can get out of them.'

'He saved Potts's life 'n' all.'

'Yeah, *I'm* glad this case is over, too, Titch.'

'Ay. It's made me feel funny.'

'It's cos nothing is what it seems, Titch.'

'That's it, Sam. Including me! I'm pretending all the time.'

'Not with me you're not.'

'No, not with you.'

'Do you think the others know?'

'Don't care if they do.'

'Nor me.'

They smiled at each other. Titch reached for her

shoulder bag and took out the packet of letters from her uncle in Calcutta, and began to read the worn pages. Sam leafed through one of his medical books. They felt very close. They felt no need to speak.

Sherlock Holmes was bored. He had arrived back from Liechtenstein, flushed with triumph following the successful conclusion of a blackmail case involving the Crown Prince, only to find 221b Baker Street deserted. According to Mrs Hudson, the Doctor had left earlier for Pentonville, but Holmes was frustrated because he had no one to share his success with. His aggravation was increased by the headline in the evening newspaper: SCOTLAND YARD INSPECTOR IN MAJOR CRIME HAUL!

The article beneath went on to outline how Lord Quentin Scarsbury had been arrested for stealing the Rose of Africa from the Aston family: achieved in cooperation with the South African Police, this was being heralded as a superlative example of international collaboration. Edward Aston had been brought to justice for the murders of the Shift Manager in the vaults of the African Diamond Company in Mayfair and a Mr Charvis of Cripplegate Square. In addition, Scotland Yard's heroic endeavours had led to the apprehension of the international adventuress Irene Adler, who was awaiting trial for her part in the theft of the Rose, which had been found in her possession. Holmes read, to his mounting disgust, that behind all these successes was the mastermind, Inspector Lestrade of Scotland Yard. Regaining the stolen diamond was seen as the jewel in the crown of Lestrade's extraordinary personal triumph, but it was his capture of Irene Adler which most irked Holmes.

He slung the newspaper to the ground. 'Lestrade,' he cried, 'could not outwit Irene Adler in a thousand years! Lestrade could not outwit a teapot! I know who is behind this! The Irregulars!' He threw himself dejectedly on to the sofa. 'Lestrade a mastermind?' he moaned. 'Poppycock!'

# DR WATSON'S DIARY –
# AN UNPUBLISHED FRAGMENT

Well, in spite of my fears, all seems to be well. Irene Adler has been charged, and can look forward to a stiff sentence. Scarsbury is still in hospital, but as soon he is out, he is to be extradited to South Africa to face trial. Uncle Hector is back home – and, according to young Potts, is happily bashing away at his tambourine again! Lestrade has become intolerably pompous, and has quite forgotten that he owes it all to Sam and the Irregulars. Holmes is bored out of his mind, and thoroughly disgruntled, obsessing about Professor Moriarty, whom he fears is still working on some heinous crime of monstrous proportions.

According to my friend, Billy is making great progress in 'otelery, as Potts calls it. What a character

Potts is – a real survivor. Titch now has a small boat. We are doing everything we can to prolong Edie's eyesight. Sam is harder to read – very private boy – but I think he liked the notion of working at my surgery; that way I can train him up and perhaps get him into a medical college if he is really serious about a career in medicine, which he appears to be. I have become damnably attached to these children, and I flatter myself that they are fond of me – they made my birthday most memorable. And when I got back to Baker Street that evening, I had forgotten that there was a present from them waiting for me.

On the hall table was an envelope, with a lump in it. I felt it first to see if I could guess what it was, but it was no good, I had to open it. Inside there were three things! The first was a birthday card – cheap tosh, but obviously Sam and Titch had bought it themselves. In it Sam had written – in his increasingly decent fist – *With love and thanks from All The Baker Street Irregulars!* – which makes it of great sentimental value.

The lump turned out to be a jewel – a pink diamond! This I take to be the counterfeit Rose that Sam retrieved from dear old Ruben Curtis. But the third object is extraordinary. How they came by it, I have yet to enquire. Folded into the card was a lace handkerchief. Most delicate thing. I shall treasure it as a memento of the day I assisted in the arrest of Irene Adler. It reminded me of her pearl-handled pistol, because in the corner, embroidered in pink silk, were the initials: I.A.

**Read on for more Baker Street Mysteries in**
*The Shadow of Evil*
**coming soon . . .**

A cab drew up outside the wall by the Bastion Tower. Through the postern gate came the instantly recognisable figure of 'Tiger' De Ville – a tree of a man with unnaturally long arms and enormous hands. With huge strides, De Ville stalked round the cab, checking the area for security. He returned to the gate, and ushered through it a man with a large bald dome of a forehead. His face was white. He had an aura about him. He moved slowly, deliberately. Sam was mesmerised. Holmes had warned him that he might also see Professor Moriarty. De Ville led the evil Professor to the cab, and watched as the horse pulled off.

When the cab was safely under way, De Ville whipped round unexpectedly and looked straight at Sam. Stunned by the intense glare in De Ville's savage eyes, Sam flinched. De Ville walked towards him. His brow was deep-lined, and he had a bushy handlebar moustache. He moved fast, and as he came closer, Sam realised how he had come by the nickname 'Tiger' – his grey hair contained two streaks of black, running in a V from the centre of his forehead.

'Don't move, kid. Stay right where you are!' De Ville growled.

Before Sam could gather his things and run for it, De Ville was on him. One mighty hand clawed his shoulder, and forced him to the ground. De Ville stamped his foot on Sam's shoe box. 'If you're here to shine shoes, kid, get shining.' Kneeling, trying to conceal his shaking fingers, Sam applied a great blob of polish to De Ville's massive leather shoes. 'And don't clog the lace-holes,' De Ville snarled. Under his intimidating glare, Sam shone the boots in silence. When he was nearly done, De Ville asked, 'What's business like at this hour, kid?'

'Not great, sir,' mumbled Sam mumbled, keeping his head down.

'I bet it isn't.'

'But I don't have nowhere to go for home, so I stay here.'

'Rubbish. You don't fool me, kid. You or your mates.'

The hairs on Sam's neck stood on end – De Ville had obviously been observing *him*. He sensed De Ville watching him now, as he buffed up the shine.

'That'll do,' said De Ville, whipping his foot away. Sam put his brushes and duster away clumsily, frightened of what De Ville would do next.

'Get up, kid.'

Sam rose nervously. De Ville's feral eyes fixed him. His mouth was wide. At each side, long, tobacco-stained teeth protruded, reinforcing the image of the tiger. There was a glint of gold from between his thick, shiny lips. De Ville's hand shot out, encircling Sam's throat and pinning him to the wall. His thumb pushed Sam's head to one side. Sam could feel the thick hair on the back of De Ville's hand brushing the underside of his chin. But what really chilled his blood was De Ville's ample moustache. De Ville leant forward, bringing his lips close to Sam's ear, scratching the side of his neck with his whiskers, reminding him of the black underwater phantom of his dreams, whose bristles he could feel, even as it strangled him.

'I am known as Tiger,' breathed De Ville. 'Can you guess why?' Sam shook his head. 'Because I sleep with one eye open, kid. Like a tiger. And I shall always have one eye open for you. Get it?' Sam grunted. De Ville was so close Sam could smell the pungent odour of cigar on his breath and clothes. De Ville's rough tweed suit rubbed against him like a pelt. 'I don't ever want to see you again, kid,' he sneered. Sam felt enveloped by this vile-smelling, hairy creature. De Ville tightened his grip on Sam's throat and forced Sam up on to his toes.

'Here or anywhere. Get it?' Sam struggled to nod, but couldn't. He tried to speak, but he couldn't. Suddenly De Ville loosened his stranglehold. Sam's knees buckled and he clutched his aching throat. 'Scarper.' Forgetting his shoe box, Sam ran for it. He didn't look round. He didn't need to. He could feel De Ville's eyes burning into his back. He knew the man was after him. He could hear the slap of his boots. Just like his dream.

It is nearly five miles from the Tower of London to Baker Street. Sam ran every yard of it, but it was not until he nipped out of Soho Square and crossed Oxford Street that he felt he could relax. Still cautious, he engineered his way through some of the obscurer crannies around Wimpole Street. By the time he reached Marylebone Road, he sensed he was out of danger, but not for one moment did he slacken his pace, legging it past Madame Tussaud's into that short neck of road between Baker Street Railway Station and the corner of Regent's Park, where Sherlock Holmes and Dr Watson had rooms. There, on the first floor of 221b, Sam saw a light burning in the study, and finally, he felt safe. Still looking back at the street, he raised the heavy brass doorknocker.

Despite the late hour, Sam's friend Billy Chizzell, the

pageboy, opened the door. Sam stood, panting, unable to speak.

'You all right?' Billy said, welcoming his friend. 'Come down to the kitchen and cool off.' He chattered on. 'Mrs Hudson's gone to bed. We can have the place to ourselves.' Sam fell into the hall, put his hands on his knees and struggled to get his breath back. 'Close the door, Sam. It's turning nippy.'

As he pushed the door to, Sam just managed to spit out the words, 'Is Mr Holmes back?'

'No. Sorry.' Putting two and two together was not Billy's forte, but he suddenly realised *why* Sam was in a state. 'Oh, crikey! Have you got news?' Sam nodded. 'Wow! Brilliant!' cried Billy, clapping his hands.

'No word from Mr Holmes, though?' Sam gasped.

'No!'

'Then I must speak to Dr Watson.'

'He's got someone with him – some American – Mr J. Wilson Booth blooming Senior. Just barged in – well after hours if you ask me! They're up there now, and between you and me, it doesn't sound as though it's going too well. Listen.'

As they climbed the stairs Sam became aware of voices raised so loud, that even from the landing outside the study door, he and Billy could hear what was being said.

'I had a contract with Mr Holmes, Doctor . . .' the voice was deep and resonant, with a rich Texan drawl.

'With respect, sir,' Watson interjected, 'Holmes has never used formal contracts.'

'A Gentleman's Agreement then,' the speaker snarled gruffly. 'Your Mr Holmes undertook to protect my company's ships from sabotage. And what does he do? Disappear. Since he shook my hand he has been hiding from me, Dr Watson, and you know where.'

Watson had a pretty good idea where Holmes was, but he had been sworn to secrecy. All he could do was assure Mr J. Wilson Booth Senior that Holmes was a man of his word. From the landing, the two boys could hear Watson blustering away.

Billy looked at Sam. 'It sounds to me as though the old Doc needs helping out in there!'

'I don't think it would help if we went in now, Billy,' said Sam, who just about had his breath back.

Before either of them could do anything, the study door opened, and Mr Booth came storming out. He was a large man. Tall. Broad. He wore a linen suit whose expert tailoring instantly displayed its owner's wealth, and a Texan leather cord tie, held at the neck by a chunky bull-horn clasp. This imposing figure was stopped in his tracks, not by Billy, whom he continued to ignore as he had when he arrived, but by the sight of Sam – a grubby, sweating street urchin, in tattered clothes. He simply stood and gaped.

'Sam here was waiting to see Dr Watson,' said Billy with a grin. 'Have you finished?' Booth was flabbergasted by Billy's cheek, but it didn't take him long to find his tongue. 'Out of my way, you ragamuffins!' he cried, charging past the two boys, brandishing his Stetson hat. As he descended the stairs he called out, 'Dr Watson, you will be hearing from my attorney.'

Watson appeared in the study doorway looking somewhat deflated. Holmes was always putting him in situations like this. But, as Sam had observed before, Watson never complained – his loyalty was unquestioning.

Sam looked at the dejected doctor. 'Where *is* Mr Holmes, Doctor?'

'Don't you start, Wiggins!' replied Watson.

As he made his way along the hall, Mr Booth overheard Sam. 'That's a damned perspicacious question, young whippersnapper,' he called out, 'And one to which I too would like an answer! Where *is* Mr Holmes?'

Leaning over the banisters, and addressing the fiery American fuming in the hall below, Watson shrugged apologetically. 'At this moment, Mr Booth, I am unable to answer your question.' Watson was quite pleased with this truthful evasion, but it was too much for Mr J. Wilson Booth Senior. Planting his Stetson firmly on his head, and flourishing his cane, he strode to the front door.

'That's a dashed slippery answer, Dr Watson. You are no gentleman, sir, and your Mr Holmes is a charlatan! A charlatan and a phoney! Good night.' So saying, he slammed the door.

'And good night to you too, Mr Booth,' said Billy under his breath.

Sam looked at Watson. 'Was it something I said?'

Watson smiled fondly at his two young friends. 'Come in here. Tell me your news. And I will tell you all about Mr J. Wilson Booth Senior.' Watson ushered them into the study. 'It is quite a story!'